P9-CFA-285

BY ANNE RICHARDSON ROIPHE

DIGGING OUT

UP THE SANDBOX!

UP THE SANDBOX!

ANNE RICHARDSON ROIPHE

SIMON AND SCHUSTER · NEW YORK

All rights reserved
including the right of reproduction
in whole or in part in any form

Copyright © 1970 by Anne Richardson Roiphe

Published by Simon and Schuster
Rockefeller Center, 630 Fifth Avenue
New York, New York 10020

Second printing

SBN 671-20704-0

Library of Congress Catalog Card Number: 79-130488

Designed by Eve Metz

Manufactured in the United States of America

FOR MARGARET

UP THE SANDBOX!

IN WEEK ONE

After the children's nap, I repeated the morning's chores in an abbreviated fashion. I took chicken out of the freezer compartment for dinner. I smoothed the bed. I changed the baby and I yelled at Elizabeth for pulling the petals off my white geranium, its blossom now picked and scabby, tilting to one side. It sits on the window sill next to a cellophane bag of half-consumed chocolate cookies, looking, I suppose, as if it belongs to us. Suddenly I am in a hurry to get out of the apartment. The brick wall behind the kitchen window lets in no light. The dishes in the sink seem unbearable and the spilled orange juice on the counter surface seems a defacement, like obscenities scrawled in lipstick on public monuments. The early June heat and the garbage, not entirely contained within the aluminum can, combine in a terrible odor.

We rush out the door, barely remembering pail and shovel, money for ice cream. In the dark hallway at first I feel relieved. It's cooler, the dampness and draft are stored in the green-painted cement walls and as in a cave there is the chill of objects untouched by sun or open air—a sense of bats and mice and snakes that hide, cool under the rocks. I hold Elizabeth close, and ring again and again for the elevator, which lumbers its way up to the sixth floor. The door slides open, and then before I can insert the stroller, the gray steel slabs move quickly shut and we jump back. The unthinking machine, responding to another call, would chop our hands off, decapitate the children, and crush us in its unrelenting need to obey an electronic impulse. Slowly it creeps to the tenth floor. I watch the numbers light on the plaque above the door. I ring again and it stops in its descent. A woman, a vertical neighbor, holds the proper button as I maneuver the stroller, Elizabeth and myself inside. She releases the button; the door groans and shuts. We stare at the panel of lights telling us of our slow progress downward, as if a message were being sent and only with total concentration can we decipher the code. At last the first floor. The lady holds the "open" button as I lead Elizabeth and the baby out. We hurry through the yellow lobby.

• • •

At last out in the sunshine. Hit by the sudden heat and light, Peter cries and pulls at his thin hair. The motion of the carriage soothes him and we cross Broadway, quiet in the early afternoon. A truck is delivering rolls to a bakery down the block, a few children are jumping rope outside the laundry, and the dwarf lady who lives in our building is hurrying across the street, her shopping bag filled, her fat legs bare and her feet encased in their usual heavy orthopedic shoes. Her face is round and her features are broad, distorted by thick glasses. I had never seen a dwarf till we moved to this building. It's been four years now, and each time we pass my skin crawls. Despite all the humane teachings I have of course heard, I still feel not considerate, compassionate or easy in the company of cripples. I hold to the medieval conviction that someone has been criminal, perhaps in bed, or maybe only in imagination, but someone has committed a crime, perhaps the victim herself.

I push the carriage into the park; my dress is stained with perspiration. The heat muffles the street sounds and the green leaves and the grass seem so pleasant, I am glad to be here in the park. There are other mothers in the playground. It's still early and many benches are free. A child runs to the concrete fountain and by leaning with all his weight against a metal button embedded in the grainy cement produces a trickle of cool water that bubbles erratically above the metal spout. He gets his shirt all wet trying to position his mouth correctly and finally gets down, walks to his mother's side. She talks to the mother on the bench next to her about a badminton club in Brooklyn where she and her husband happily release their accumulated aggressions. I look around at the pull toys, the hoop and the roller skates that lie just beneath the bench next to mine. They have in themselves, these objects of commercial greed, mass-produced wonder and childhood lust, a curious beauty in the shade beneath the bench, like shells on the shore, emptied of their inner life.

I pick up my baby and hold him on my lap. He looks up at my face, his fingers exploring my mouth, digging at my nose. What stays on, what comes off—I can see him wondering. I could starve him—or leave him behind me, dropping him on the cement, crying in the park till the police come and assign him some nameless future. But he has nothing to fear because, despite an angry thought or two, we are connected deeply and permanently. And with each feeding, each soothing, each moment we live together, I grow into him. My spirit oozes out, I feel myself contracting and him expanding, and the ties between us solidify. And I am almost his possession. Elizabeth's, too. My selfish purposes are also served, as the children make for me a universe, with a design and a rhythm and a function. And instead of being, as I was before I conceived a child, a bit of dark matter orbiting aimlessly, brooding on my own molecular disintegration, I am now a proper part of ordinary society.

I think of Paul in the library now, probably in one of the study cubicles, with its desk piled with documents on the Spanish Civil War. He said he was looking for testimony, reports from the original members of the Abraham Lincoln Brigade. I know the way his hair hangs across his face when he reads, the way he chews on his fingernails and screws up his eyes when he detects dishonesty or distortion in his text. I wish somehow I could be with him—the days seem so long when he's absorbed that way—as if I didn't matter, as if the children were peripheral noise, as if his scholarship and theories were food sufficient. And then I get sad, because nothing I have ever read or done, nothing I will ever learn or speculate about, can replace being near him. I would put anything down to go for a short walk with him. There is a terrible inequality of love in that, and I am so reduced. I am like the heroine bound and gagged by the villain, lying on the railroad tracks, waiting for her rescuer. He comes, releases her, kissing the tears away. Only he leaves, this hero with many interests, and the villain returns, and the scene must be repeated over and

over. The metaphor is melodramatic. Actually, Paul and I
exist in a more ordinary way. We live, not like explorers, not
like Lewis and Clark charting the wilds of the northwest;
more like land surveyors blocking out lots for a new housing
project or a county shopping center. The possibilities for raw
adventure under such circumstances are limited.

Two students walk by, peering between the playground
bars. They still feel about public events as if they could mold
them like the clay that used to yield beneath their fingers in
art classes in elementary school afternoon programs. They go
to the barricades, hair flying, jaws set, to reform a system
whose basic injustices are beyond reach, hidden and perpetual. They list grievances of representation, scholarships, draft,
university alliances with military matters, and they shake the
ground on which they stamp their feet, and their catcalls are
reported in the press, and the drama around here is great. And
above them and below them, the web stays. The fabric vibrates
like a trampoline, bouncing us in somersaults we execute with
more or less grace. And the same words are said by different
people over and over. The students move on to look at other
interesting sights in the park.

If I were younger, I would join the student revolutionaries.
If Paul were just a few years younger, he would have had his
head bashed in on the principle of student power. As it is,
Elizabeth needs a daily bath and other things, and the baby
must have what the books call consistent mothering or his
small soul will warp and bend in strange directions, and he
might decide it's not worth growing and reverse the process,
curl himself in fetal position and look only inward, refusing
food until life itself is extinguished. And so with my hands,
when I touch him and wipe the cereal from his face and the

b.m. from his bottom, I make life again each day, like Penelope weaving a shroud, never to be complete till Ulysses returns. I wonder, if I were Penelope, if I should not have smuggled myself aboard the ship originally headed for Troy. Or if perhaps, even now, I should not accept the hot kisses of some impatient suitor who would rape me on the hills and carry me off to a different city where the language itself would be unknown to me.

I'm no Penelope, no romantic heroine or creature of historical importance. I'm just Margaret Reynolds, wife and mother, not yet thirty . . . too old for an identity crisis and yet not past the age of uncertainty. . . . I grew up like all the other ordinary field flowers on an ordinary hill in a nice suburb and my daddy was a nice accountant-daddy who counted the money in counting houses of several corporations conveniently located in nearby Newark and I had a dog of no particular breed and a mother who played cards with her lady friends in the afternoon and solitaire alone on the couch waiting for my father to come home in the evening. The only distinguished thing that happened to me was that my father had a coronary in his office when I was twelve and died very quickly, to the shock of his partners and his small family. I was left with a perfectly unchanged life, because my daddy had been prudent, but I developed a concern over questions that didn't unduly trouble my playmates and friends. When I went to Barnard and found I was a garden-variety girl . . . I became comfortable in my surroundings and vowed I would live in the city the rest of my life . . . crossing the river back only on such occasions as last Sunday, when we were supposed to go to my mother's in New Jersey. . . .

An aunt's birthday was to be celebrated on the lawn. My

mother had hired a caterer and little tables with candy-striped cloths, and pink carnations were going to be scattered over the grass. Paul never complains about this sort of event, taking the gruesome exposure to my family in his stride. I for my part cringe under the glaring eyes of relatives who stare at me as though I were some abnormality. They compare my state in life with that of their own children, and they gloatingly tell sad stories of my promising youth. My mother winces because my shoes or clothes are wrong, my hair unwashed, or Elizabeth's dress too short. Across the George Washington Bridge there is a world of disapproval, a native tribe whose customs are inviolable, and defectors, members who have snuck off to the bush, are—if apprehended—shown no mercy. We would have gone, nevertheless, to my aunt's birthday party, but the night before had sapped us of all our strength and we spent the day in bathrobes, with the shades pulled down, reading and rereading the fine print in the Sunday *Times*.

On the way home from the park I stopped in at Woolworth's. Elizabeth loves the five-and-dime, the hamsters turning on their wheels in tiny cages, the goldfish swimming in tanks along the far wall, the rack of dog chains and cat trays, the birdseed and the sickly parakeets all dazzling in their unspoken promise of possession. Elizabeth also likes the ribbon rack, the nail polish counter, and the rows of plastic dolls and birthday-party paper hats and plates. I am always tempted by such a display. I fight the urge to fill my basket with safety pins, and cotton balls, and hair-bows and colored aprons and rainhats, and up and down the rows I prowl—with ten dollars I could almost gratify all the longings I suddenly have, but that would be immoral. Beyond the expense, it would be improper. I am an American Puritan, and no sentence in the stockades would be long enough to ever expiate all my sins. I settled on two chocolate brownies and a package of rubber pants, and I bought Elizabeth a little box of crayons and a coloring book with outlined pictures of elephants and tigers.

When we got home, I rested for a moment in the stuffed armchair Paul's father had given us as a wedding present. It came from the parlor of his house in Stockbridge and had become our favorite possession. We had driven down in a borrowed station wagon and the chair had been shoved in the back on end, like a great sea turtle overturned. We had sat next to each other on the front seat and I had felt a kind of exhilaration as if the chair were our homestead and signaled the beginning of the plowing and the fencing of the land. I touched him, rubbed against him, hindered his driving, fondled the hair on the back of his neck, and I was so hot and moist and charged with irrepressible willfulness that somewhere in northern Connecticut he was forced to pull the car off the highway, onto a more personal back road with trees arching overhead, a farm in the distance, and a diner half a mile beyond. There in the dark we lay in the back of the station wagon, zigzagging our bodies around the immovable chair. Then we had greasy grilled cheese sandwiches in the diner. I fell asleep the last part of the trip. He was whistling a Bach aria and I knew he was pleased.

When I got up from the chair, I undressed the baby and bathed him in the tub. I powdered him and put on his flannel nightgown, unpressed but clean. He and I were talking to each other, the mass of happy sounds probably preferable to speech and all the concomitant woe that comes with long sentences and exchanged opinions. I had left Elizabeth in the living room playing with her crayons and her new book. As soon as I had the baby settled, I called her for her bath. I helped her undress and splashed the water for her and soaped the park dirt off. I looked at her small body, a vagina so smooth and hidden, the tiny clitoris still white, like a marble statue, so unlike my hairy mound, so unlike my full labia and the pulsating, discharging, odorous, membranous opening, scarred by two episiotomies (a slight scar—I needed a magnifying mirror to notice it). If I looked very closely I could see the soft blond fuzz on Elizabeth's mound that would one day grow thick and bushy, covering the oozy changes that would go on below. I felt sad somehow that we couldn't preserve the sculptured perfection of our own immature genitals. I washed behind her ears and we talked about the rather sticky subject of baby lambs and lamb chops, one of her favorite foods. Different animals eat each other up, that's just the way it is, I said. And I saw reflected on her young face the same moral shock, the unbelieving righteousness, that had gripped my mother when years ago I had explained that no one in my college dormitory was a virgin, no exceptions at all. I was gleeful in that revelation to my mother, but felt embarrassed by Elizabeth's stare, and somehow compromised by my indifference to the fate of baby lambs.

Paul came home. I heard the thud of the briefcase and felt the quickening of my mind, a kind of lightening as in the last weeks of pregnancy when the baby slips down and it's suddenly easier to breathe, a relief. I rushed to the mirror and patted my hair and tucked the errant strands into the proper clip. I looked for my powder but couldn't find it, probably having left it in the kitchen in the morning. He had worked hard; his eyes had that dazed look of a man returning from a long trip. He admired Elizabeth's new coloring book and held the baby while I prepared the children's supper. He wandered about the apartment picking up toys that had scattered, a comb that had fallen under the bed. He likes things to be in better order than I seem to be able to keep them. I know what there is to be done and still I have trouble.

Eat, eliminate, prepare food, clean up, shop, throw out the garbage, a routine clear as a geometric form, a linear pattern that seems almost graceful in its simplicity. Despite computers and digit telephone numbers, nuclear fission, my life hardly differs from that of an Indian squaw settled in a tepee on the same Manhattan land centuries ago. Pick, clean, prepare, throw out, dig a hole, bury the waste—she was my sister. She would understand why there should be one day of total fast each week.

The disaster started innocently enough, after the children were in bed and I was starting to heat the chicken for us. Paul was collecting his notes for tomorrow's work in the library when he found a page of neatly written quotes from Robespierre attacking the ambitions of Danton. The page had been done months ago and held for probable use in his chapter on the French revolutionaries. Diabolical madmen all, was what he was saying. The page had been thickly crayoned on in heavy bold purple and green strokes. Elizabeth had made circles, aimless lines, a possible stick figure with frizzy hair that sprawled across the bottom of the page. Most of the words themselves, collected from many sources, were now obliterated by thick crayon. It must have happened while I was bathing the baby. He turned pale, and I knew at that second how the following hours would go. His lips formed quickly into a thin line and his eyes went dead. "You let this happen.

You let her destroy my work paper. You just casually without
a thought allowed her to crayon on my paper. You might just
as well give her a paintbrush, let her do the walls. Or a scis-
sors. Why not give her the rest of my manuscript to make
paper dolls?" And he turned his back, controlling a terrible
stream of invective. He threw himself down in our armchair,
a thick wall of fury blocking my access. And although I tried
not to let it happen, I felt myself crumble, my adult, womanly,
maternal self dissolve before a cloud of childhood guilt, of
vases broken, milk spilt at the table, arithmetic homework not
handed in, misspelled words, messy bureau drawers, grape
juice stains on party dresses—a sense of abandonment, alone-
ness, a need for my bed, my pillow, sanctuary, a place where
under the covers my hands could rub on my own body till,
somewhat eased, I could fitfully sleep, forgetting the furies I
had aroused. In numbness I finished the dishes, and when I
looked at him again, he was sitting rigid in the chair, as if the
outer edges of his body were the silent streets just beyond the
bombed-out area of the city. Those buildings whose founda-
tions were rocked by the nearby blast seemed to hold themselves taut, so they too will not turn to rubble, meaningless
formless piles of chipped and broken stone. So he sat in the
chair and glared at me. He didn't speak, and I didn't dare. I
knew ultimately this issue would end. I reassured myself with
thoughts of other early morning reconciliations, and it was
true, I was careless, I did allow the children to strew the
apartment with the litter of their activities. I had permitted
milk stains to blotch the rug, I had myself burned a cigarette
hole in the couch cover. There were odds and ends of posses-
sions all out of order, in irregular and unmanageable places.
The chores each day, if I faced their demands, were over-

whelming, and only by laxity, a certain bohemian looseness, was I able to keep us all together. Sometimes I wanted my mother and her maid to come and take care of it all. I fairly screamed out for home, for the days when the ultimate mess was undreamed of and marriage seemed a game of picking out a trousseau and addressing thankyou notes to relatives for lovely presents that came wrapped in tissue paper that someone else threw out.

At last Paul got up and without a word left the apartment; martyred, he slammed the door behind him, and when I stood at the bedroom window I could see him walking down Broadway. I could see fatigue in his posture. Where would he go without me—to an art movie at the Thalia, a double feature of grade D Westerns at Loew's, a Spanish love story in an uptown movie house? Would he go to a bar, or the park; would he call a friend and hike across the George Washington Bridge? Other more lurid images I pushed away. I could only follow his back till it disappeared from view and I knew all the while he was regretting the day he met me.

I went in to check on Elizabeth. She was quiet and eager for privacy or sleep, as if she needed refuge from the electricity he and I had discharged. I pulled the armchair—our armchair—over to the window. I tried to read Anthony Trollope—perhaps the boils of English society, gently lanced, would soothe me.

Slowly, with skillful hand, the picture built of lovely estates and gracious characters beset with the problems of ordinary English life. My restlessness grew. I needed a more violent story, one of my own century. I picked up a paperback copy of a biography of Christine Jorgensen, the man who had been changed to a woman by clever surgery—courtesy of modern

Sweden. The story started with the little boy surprised in the act of trying on his mother's brassiere and panties. I couldn't concentrate. Someday maybe they would make a pill, no nasty operation necessary, and everyone could choose a sexual identity, and perhaps switch back and forth at different stages of life. If I was angry with my husband, I could spite him the ultimate spite and change my sex so that he could no longer claim my passive attending love. I would not be waiting at the window while he stalked out into the night. But then I thought about it more graphically. To have that incredible member grafted on, swelling and shrinking and hanging about, dangling between my legs—how would I walk or sit? And then I would have to give up all the pleasures that I was so used to lying outstretched on the bed with my womb silent, unfelt, but expecting, reacting, infinite in its possibilities. How could I possibly give up my body and myself, waiting for things to enter me, to travel up and down dark areas, and split and divide? The caves in my own personal labyrinth could be explored endlessly. I decided to wait for Paul and not be so very angry with him.

I saw the drugstore close and the owner pull his iron gate across the windows filled with bubble baths, lipsticks, hair brushes and inviting pictures of sultry girls sporting cosmetics that I always finally bought only to be disappointed in their effect. I watched the crowds move up and down the street—the students, male and female, arms about each other, sandals, long hair, Indian prints and tinted glasses—a style of life that fairly shouted of psychedelic secrets and rejected station wagons and homes in the country. I watched, leaning out the window on my elbows, too high to clearly make out faces, but low enough to feel the surge, the rhythm of the girls in their

Afro haircuts, men in dashikis, Puerto Rican women bulging in satin dresses, the smell of sex. I was suspended above the street like a smiling Humpty-Dumpty Macy's Day balloon, as if the strings to my shape were being held by some small men down below. I wanted to deflate, to be down there, pouring from the subway, out of the movie, stopping to stare, to eat pizza and ice cream cones, to wander in the glare of the lights.

Many hours later the avenue became quiet, an addict or two walking in slow motion, each slipping through his private fog. There was an old man exercising a dog of indiscriminate origin. The fire engines break the quiet with their shrieking sirens. A half hour later they come quietly back down the other side of Broadway. I am eager one day to see something with rich red flames burn all the way to the ground.

Later still. I am not able to sleep alone. I wait by the window. The bar on the corner releases its last boisterous patrons, who flow onto the middle of the street; with drunken bravado they shout at the occasionally passing cars. Time is no longer contained within the numbers of the clock. I am orbiting. Many years or moments may be passing. I am adrift with other lifeless matter in the solar system, and simultaneously I am listening for a sound at the front door.

At last the bell rings. He had left without his keys. He comes over to me, pale and tired, his eyes like pages in last winter's magazine left in the waiting room of a dentist. "I went to see a Betty Grable movie," he said. "You would have liked it." The anger was gone, and with his return I again felt myself complete, no longer a discarded fragment or a bit of peeling from the old paint. I was a whole, excavated treasure, an amphora waiting to be filled. We went immediately to bed, the important thing no longer the crayoned paper or his desertion, or my long night of waiting. It was now just the touch of each other, familiar and tender, exciting without being frightening. Suddenly as we slipped together I remembered I had not, not expecting him, not planning for the evening to end this way, I had not put on my diaphragm, and it was sitting on a shelf in the medicine chest where it served me not at all. I thought of saying something, of stopping us, and then decided, or perhaps more accurately gave up making a decision, and relaxed into a love that would last uninterrupted by other pressures for a short while.

We did not go out to New Jersey. I called my mother and told her Elizabeth had a cold. (A lie is a wish, I read somewhere: do I so punish Elizabeth for her crayoning on history notes?) All morning I poured coffee down us to fight the fatigue of too much feeling. Tomorrow things will be back to normal.

OUT OF WEEK ONE

At night when I walk along Riverside Drive, I look north past the last of the real estate holdings of Columbia University to the dark of Harlem, where alone, female and white, I can never go. It's like staring across a river alive with whirlpools, rapids and bumping logs, across to another country whose border guards stand with bayonets pointed outward, eager in their boredom to kill any intrusive stranger.

When I was still in junior high, I sent my allowance to the NAACP, and then I joined CORE and then SNCC. But last Tuesday, in a logical progression of despair, I was sworn in to a special group, PROWL. Their purpose is truly revolutionary, the leaders make no nice deals with the establishment, and the recruits must show their loyalty by some major act, some criminal and terrorist deed that forever submerges them into a revolutionary existence. How did I come to such an extreme? Sometimes when I am frightened I remember the pledge-allegiance-to-the-flag I said each morning at school. I remember the Fourth of July parades, the fireworks on the Jersey shore, and of course the certain sense of progress, reform and expectation that filled my early years with the sweet mingled taste of patriotism and pride. But that was self-love and delusion. Gradually I saw the poor were multiplying in their misery and the comfortable were crossly defending their land. I noticed the barbed-wire fences at the edges of my father's country club, and I saw that the safe avenues of social action, the Junior League, the local Democratic club, the settlement house, all perpetuated the very system that bound us all in shared guilt. And I knew I could allow myself no single private life separated from political context. To do so would be to collaborate with the exploiters, to aid the Nazis in rushing the Jews to the crematorium, to assist the Southern bigot in hiding needed food stamps, to join him as he dances primitive war hops around a burning cross.

It's perfectly clear to me I'm obsessed with a passion for purity, for some moral goodness I keep expecting to find or create in the world around. But I am not such a prig as that would indicate. I know how corrupt, eroded and diseased I am—malignant galloping growths settling in my soul the same as everyone else's.

Take for example the black problem. When I was a child and had fears at night of a strange man climbing up on our porch, shinnying up the drainpipe, clinging to the first-story ledge and crawling to my window, opening it and holding me at knife-point, victim of some unnamable, unpicturable desires, that intruder was never blond and blue-eyed. Always as I enacted the scene over and over again, hands shaking beneath the covers I had pulled tight against my body, the man was brown-skinned, kinky-haired, wide nostrils, flat lips, dark skin, dark deeds, sneaking through the black night. The

shadows of the alleys behind the supermarket, the corners
of the library in high school—who might be there menacing
me with a blackjack and a cold look of hatred? Not a Scandi-
navian, a German, an Italian, only a black man, emissary of
Satan, charred in the devil's own fire. Such stupid thoughts,
such unacceptable rubbish—a race myth, in the modern mind
of an emancipated child. But how to burn it out—to purify
one's mind of worms and grubs and frights of strangers, and a
fear of the black Walpurgisnacht, when all the demons will
run loose over the suburban lawns saying "You must now be
slaves. Take your turn. It's only fair. The master must grovel
in the dirt." I mean to say that despite my concern for civil
liberties, for equality, for justice in Mississippi and freedom
in Alabama and school busing in Massachusetts—I am blond,
and blond is still beautiful, and if I have one life to lead it
will be as a white, and I am a mass of internal contradictions,
all of which cause me to finally attempt some rite which will
bring salvation, save me from a system I despise but still carry
within me like any other of my vital organs.

And now, although I seem an ordinary housewife, I have
assumed another identity, a counter-personality. I feed my
husband and children, and then at odd hours, on pretexts as
yet accepted by them all, I meet with my other friends in the
room John has rented at 110th and Amsterdam, and we plan
and talk and drink beer, and anticipate with mingled terror
and joy the apocalypse, the day of judgment, the confrontation of poor and rich, black and white, and I envision the
American redemption, the resurrected black souls of Harlem
floating over the luxury dwellings of the city, some tenderly
forgiving their enemies, others name calling and spitting great

27

accumulations of saliva on the heads of their now humbled adversaries. I am no longer a honky, an enemy, an alien. I have made it to the other side of the river, and I am now in a state of grace because I am counted among the depressed, not the tyrants. I am not an observer, a reader of *The New York Times*, a sympathizer with tender thoughts—I have put my body into the fight and am prepared to sacrifice everything that may be demanded. I want to mean that last, but I still have doubts about myself.

PROWL's immediate plan (conceived by Koboto, a Mau Mau from Kenya who last year held the Ford Foundation African Studies chair at Columbia) is to blow up the George Washington Bridge. John agrees that only by such an act of war, a declaration of position, can the blacks force the confrontation. From a military point of view, John says, we shall aim to isolate Manhattan and then, when there are more blacks than whites in residence here, we shall take over City Hall and claim the island for the liberation. Black solidarity will not be a ghetto school holiday, but a political reality.

There are six of us in the PROWL unit—it is sufficient for the present job. I am the *only* white. I was accepted because I have been having a relationship of a very intense and personal kind with John. Infidelity. Adultery. Sometimes I look at myself as my mother might, and I am for a moment shocked. My behavior seems bold and disgusting, but then I quickly remember I am not a part of her society but a member of my own, and our customs differ. But part of me still says, Crazy, crazy, you should be in an institution, acting like this—a year at Austen Riggs or Highlands would bring you back into the fold—fold, crush, crumple—I'll have to follow my impulses. I love my husband and would never want to hurt him or the children, but there is a certain lust left over, a capacity for more than one love at a time, a certain desire for variety that seems after all so simple to satisfy.

Is fidelity a virtue or a chain, a sign of middle-class stupidity, an unthinking bourgeois reaction? or is it lack of courage that keeps couples stuck to each other with occasional guilty thoughts at midnight? All I know is I will not be shut up in any single life-box with bolted doors. I have as much right to be a pirate, or a cowboy, or a fortune hunter as anybody else. My sex is not as limiting as people, my mother, for example, thought. And so I could not and did not prevent the intimacy that grew between John and me, based on a sharing of revolutionary views as well as on purely sexual attraction.

"I couldn't prevent" is dodging the issue, ducking behind a traditional female pose, fainting sweetly onto the chaise longue—I didn't mean that at all. I chose John—I chose to have a romantic extramarital fling—I am no man's object, to be picked up, put down, dusted off at his will. I am able to dabble in life, to taste, experiment and expand myself, test my mettle. I chose John because the adventure matched my social convictions and the moment was right.

John was the eighth child born to his parents on an Alabama farm. He was vigorous enough to survive several of the illnesses that killed off three of his brothers and one of his sisters. He was intelligent enough to loathe the very trees and earth that comprised his rural community, seeing in them no Wordsworthian beauties of nature but an implacable force like the white sheriff holding human life in contempt and smashing the hopes of men and women till they stopped thinking or planning for tomorrow. John escaped to the city and managed sufficient education to get a job as a social

worker for the New York City Welfare Department. In order
to hold this job, he was forced to practice a debilitating deceit,
an Uncle Tomism that brought him home in the evening to his
aunt's three rooms in a housing project hating himself and the
system he served. PROWL would prove to be his personal
salvation. And, as I had felt in our first conversation in the
park, he was a superb leader and a wonderful lover, the social
ironies giving just the right kind of spice to our illicit meet-
ings.

To be with John has many satisfactions, like eating forbidden candy in bed, hiding beneath the covers crumbs and
crumpled wrappers—or staying out till dawn and walking in
the deserted early morning, hearing your own footsteps in the
silence, the sound of the garbage pails you bang, your own
whistle—to make private noises that stand out like thunder-
claps in the city streets. To sleep with John gave me all those
pleasures, because, I suppose, integrationist that I am, I am
happily shocked and so is he at what can be done in a bed
across a color line. And then of course I do (I know this is
both a social and a personal perversion), I always imagine
people watching us together in bed undoing years of carefully
laid-out taboos. I see these people, approving and disapproving, and I know my female form is being used to illustrate a
point, historically, socially, politically—and that adds to my
appetite and appreciation.

Several nights before we blew the bridge, while Paul
worked on his book, believing I was visiting a college friend,
John and I lay on the striped mattress thinking our private
thoughts while our bodies embraced.

I asked John what he was thinking of. I know this is the
most indiscreet nagging unpleasant question a woman can

find, and yet I need to hear the thoughts of the man in the bed next to me. Otherwise, if the silence goes on too long, I feel a sadness seeping in and I know that like a fast-rising tide it will soon engulf me entirely.

John said he was thinking about after the revolution. If he should survive, he would certainly be both a hero and a leader, a ranking member of the new political system; and when that had been achieved, he would like a house in Great Neck or some place like it, not too far from the city, but outside the immediate dust and noise, a barbecue pit for Sunday night soul food cook-outs, a billiard table in the playroom downstairs, a washer and a dryer for his wife— maybe even a heated swimming pool. And so on he went, like a child listing his Christmas wants in a letter to Santa Claus. Dead Mail Department was where it would all end—and I smiled ruefully at myself for having expected of my black knight that he would be different from my father or his father before him. We are all consumers. Sensing a certain coolness on my part, John switched from dreams of a cozy future to the realities of our immediate revolutionary task. The young revolutionary was so much more attractive than the projected bureaucratic government official I could see blossoming that I forced myself to push out of my mind the knowledge of his future shape and absorb myself in the present, or try to. Probably because I am escaping my own imprisonments, I would have admired him more had he aspired to owning a harem of whores, or to being king of the numbers racket or becoming a Trappist monk, or a Muslim begging alms in Mecca.

John was plotting our escape route from 177th Street after the bridge had blown. I didn't want to escape too fast, and I kept telling him that he must plan it to please me. I wanted to stay and watch the bridge fall slowly into the river, high slabs of concrete, heavy cables swinging loose and dropping into the dark waters, police sirens wailing, fire engines heaving with clumsy speed to the nearest spot, all helplessly watching the towers topple, the string of lights, shattered glass, exposed wires, extinguished by the beautiful blast of the dynamite against their construction, their passage, their route out of the city to little gardens and plastic swimming pools. All the millions of cars that in an average day would stream across like a pack of lemmings would now idle in garages, choke on their own oils and rust. It was a superb idea. The terrible rhythm of things, the toll of accepting the way things are, would not be taken by us. *Crash*—the bridge broken from its moorings would float in pieces out to sea and sink like a torpedoed freighter without any glory or last farewells, just additional debris, swiss-cheesed steel at the bottom of the uninterested sea.

As I lay in bed with John, imagining our project, it seemed so exactly right, so clear—like an old-fashioned Hollywood movie, in focus, and with inevitable actions, all unconfusing and proper. Of course the night we did it, things were different. My mind, imaginative as it is, could not have predicted how that bridge would actually go and how I would feel as I watched it, and how much of me, of my own flesh, an entire finger in fact, would go with it.

Some of the others in PROWL were in love with, or at least lusted after, John. This complicated matters between us. April had studied African history at Howard and then become a kindergarten teacher in the Bronx. Her commando experience consisted only of stalling a car on the Long Island Expressway the day the World's Fair opened. Some helpful man stopped his Cadillac, fixed her engine, and took her to lunch at the Spanish Pavilion, so her protest was abandoned in flirtation. She was as much an amateur as I. She felt it criminal of John to have sexual relations with a white woman, and I suppose it was.

Maria was the gentlest of us all. She was fond of words like *beautiful* and *love*, and she worked as a chambermaid at the Plaza Hotel, which she thought we might one day blow up and build in its place a mosque or a shrine of some sort. She thought the idea of destroying the George Washington Bridge was beautiful because all the black people would hold up their heads and shout love to one another when the deed was done. She wanted a spiritual, not a carnal, relationship with John, and as much as possible, good leader that he was, he gave it to her. He called her the blacks' answer to Mother Cabrini, which made her look away in embarrassment.

The twins completed our unit. They were in their early fifties, two Pullman car porters who had made dynamite their hobby and had successfully robbed a safe or two in their day. They had joined PROWL out of idealism and boredom after the old Pennsylvania Railroad station was torn down. They bore a harsh grievance against society, triggered by the fact that they were required to turn in their uniforms at the end of their tenure. It was hard to tell them apart, even as we plotted revolution. They "yes-ma'am-ed" and "no-ma'am-ed" me, much to the discomfort and irritation of the others, and they looked on John as the young Mohammed, the young Moses come to lead them out of the desert, and they were altogether obsequious and angry they agreed to everything, except that they wanted to blow up Grand Central Station instead of the

George Washington Bridge. But they were overruled finally by the necessity for group discipline, as our small cell was after all not in charge of decision-making but merely an obedient limb of a larger unit, whose activities were coordinated and timed to promote the black position on a worldwide basis.

I had forgotten in the years I had lived as a simple housewife and mother the strong excitement of a group experience. Of course, in my early teens I had run with a gang of girls—blood sisters we were, and we spoke hours on the phone to each other, sharing secrets that tied us together to the death or at least through the ninth grade. Later, when I worked on the school newspaper and we sat around in our press room with coffee and forbidden cigarettes, planning an exposé of the student council and its corrupt treasurer, I felt that excitement again. I belonged, I was myself *and* the others. I would do anything for them and they for me. Internally we might have our differences of opinion or taste, but to the outside world we were a bloc, a nation indivisible in our common experience. I felt it also when we did the senior program my last year of high school and rehearsed into the late hours of the night, and we alone, a band of confederates, stayed in the empty school, singing and dancing together, painting scenery. I thought then that all those people were forever a part of me, like buddies in a foxhole, or men who have sailed across the sea together in a small sloop—but actually I have forgotten most of their names, and I no longer remember the lyrics to the songs, or the costumes. I do remember the spiked punch we had at the party afterwards. But this group solidarity, so ephemeral but so beautiful while it lasts, was certainly one of my major pleasures in being a member of PROWL. It didn't matter about our

34

disparate backgrounds, our complicated ulterior and exterior motives for joining. Once together, embarked on a dangerous mission, we were a group as total as any cluster of atoms, held together properly by positive and negative attractions, and in that group I felt unburdened of myself and the terrible responsibility of singleness—I was John's and April's and Maria's and the twins' charge, just as they were mine, and I can only say that I had missed deeply that feeling all these years that I had been a grown-up—a private person without blood sisters, shared experiences—just a mind and body accountable for its own actions, like a single duck flying over the marsh, the certain target of sharpshooters and sportsmen.

I am not dismissing Paul—we are together, but that does not provide immersion, or safety, like a group. It's so much like living within yourself. The two of you become an internal climate that is somehow sufficient but not safe, or beautiful, or mystical, like a group.

The night of the explosion, hotel wedding facilities were strained to the bursting point, graduation parties were sending cascades of giggling children through the streets. On the East Side, station wagons were packed for departures to country homes and summer cottage hideaways. Camp trains were leaving, buses were pulling away from the city for the Catskills, the Blue Mountains, the Jersey shore. For some the June moon just meant going down to the street, to the neighborhood bar, to the local playground, to the crumbling steps by the reeking garbage cans. For them we were blowing up the bridge—for them and for ourselves. John said it was not possible to wake each morning, brush your teeth, put on a tie and go to work and come home each night and put food in the hole and eliminate that food and release some semen and go to sleep and wake up in the morning and repeat the patterns; he said it was not possible to ignore other people, that one had to bear witness, at least to curse and yell and go down dying with a screaming, so that someone, somewhere, would know that not all the human beings had been mixed in with the tar and steamrollered out to nothing. The only answer, John believes, is demolition and terror. I agree. There are ugly crustations on our souls, years of scum and crud hardened into terrible patterns. Only blasting it away will reveal a clean new surface on which we can build. Terrorists, madmen absorbed in their cause, have always been the most effective catalysts for social change.

That is why we drove to 177th Street, the entrance to both the upper and lower levels of the George Washington Bridge. The city seemed so quiet, and the lights of the bridge flickered gently like fireflies in a meadow. I looked down Riverside Drive, past Grant's Tomb and the Soldiers and Sailors Monument, and saw the old houses, two-dimensional from a distance, like a mural of city life done by a fourth grade class in its social studies project, like a stage set for an old musical comedy written to entertain tired businessmen. John and I had talked before of dying in valor and of our belief that time was relative. We agreed that to die in your twenties in one electric moment was better than to dwindle on into the eighties, arranging and rearranging meaningless designs to fill the days. We were prepared to complete our living that night.

And death seemed like a romantic fulfillment, like a goal almost to be reached for, not avoided, as if in dying together we would be able to maintain the union our mission gave us. It seemed important to die with purpose and pride and sadness. I imagined the funeral: an oration by Mrs. Coretta King, in

which she forgave us our violence and praised our courage
and selflessness; my mother weeping tears of non-understand-
ing; the entire College of Barnard rising silent, honoring their
dead sister; Paul, greeting our friends, bewildered but not a
little proud of his sudden notoriety. Would he then console
himself with some Barnard babysitter who would begin by
preparing meals, then take over the laundry and the arranging
of his notes? And as I thought more and more specifically
along these lines, I decided that if it was at all possible I
would try to survive the night. And I reminded myself I
would not attend this lovely funeral, as I would be cold,
stinking dead in a box in the ground.

We parked the car on a dark side street and made our way
to the upper-level entrance of the bridge, casually, as if we
were out for an evening stroll. Within ten minutes I was
walking across the upper level holding the wires that the twins
had given me, following instructions to drape them around
every second pole. I felt not as fully alive as I had expected at
such a dramatic time, but groggy and lost and silent inside,
more like I had felt when coming out of the ether after a
rather sudden tonsillectomy at the age of eight.

My mood gradually changed. I spun my share of the wires
carefully around every other cable, twice around the larger
ones, just as I had been instructed; I did it like the basket
weaving I had learned in my Girl Scout troop. I had also
learned from the same friendly leader how to knit and how to
sew on a button and make a puppet from yarn and an old
sock. The handicrafts of childhood crowded in my memory;
the memories came of potholders, bookends, clay elephants
with broken trunks, ashtrays glazed in bright running colors, a
lanyard, a wallet stitched in red plastic—all leading to an

ultimate future of needlepoint cushions to decorate my home, baby sweaters for grandchildren and other things a lady might do in the boredom of her bedroom to fight off the feeling of a machine mass-produced superfluousness. But now at last my hands—without any real skills or fine controls—were performing a task that would result in a terrifically noticeable product, the destruction of an engineering marvel, the undoing of a technological wonder. I was awed by my hands holding and threading the dangerous wires. I felt euphoric for a while, at last to be an activist, not a dreamer, a defender of others, not a well-wisher, an audience, critical or appreciative. Now I was it, in the center, on the stage, a member of the cast, standing up and being counted. I had a voice, and my voice would say No, the insanity cannot continue. Boom Boom, my voice would say, projecting so much further than my soprano had ever dared go before.

April moved across the other side of the bridge, draping wires in line with mine. Her black figure seemed so fragile, as if a strong wind would blow her over the railing and into the Hudson moving fast and dirty below.

In the shadows April bent down to string a wire close to the road surface. I couldn't see her for a moment, and then a light reflected in her hair. I suddenly remembered the poisonous sea urchins with prickly spines I had seen on the floor of the Caribbean when Paul and I had honeymooned in St. Thomas. Was I frightened of April? I took a second to wonder, then became re-engrossed in wire-curling.

John was working with boxes and dynamite sticks, carrying them to the twins, who rushed about with a kind of peculiar gait caused by the belts they were wearing from which dangled all kinds of odd-shaped tools. No cars crossed the bridge, no police came by to see what we were doing. The six of us were the sole possessors of the last moments of the bridge. Maria's job was to stay in the car and drive us away, but she was not a very disciplined person and rushed onto the bridge, writing in lipstick over the poles and on the walk: *Black is Beautiful; God is black, God is love, Black is Beautiful.* Her eyes shone and her serene face reflected a kind of joy I have never and will never know. John kept shouting to her to get back in the car, but she was listening to some higher authority, and at last he gave in, letting her rush about with her lipstick. We worked for about an hour and a half, and the sky was beginning to lighten, turning the black to ash with the promise of coming dawn.

I was afraid the commuters would start coming up the turnpikes and parkways and we would be seen by the sleepy tollhouse men.

It appeared to be ready. The twins had attached the dynamite in just the right places of stress to karate the bridge and topple the whole structure. We met at the Jersey side where Maria had parked the car. We smoked a cigarette and John, intense and shining with the pleasures of his extraordinary work, was just complimenting us all on our thoroughness, when a solitary figure brushed past, a derelict or a drug addict, a man in his fifties with a face that seemed like a gingerbread cookie, pounded into flatness with raisins for eyes and nose and mouth. The man, his shirt collar open, walked to the middle of the bridge and climbed on a rail. "Get off," we yelled. "Come back here." "Come any closer and I'll jump," he called in a stage voice, because he was the sort of man whose dramatic moments were borrowed from afternoon television shows. John called out, "We're going to blow the bridge. Come down from there." "Great," yelled the man. "Blow me with it." Time was not on the side of stalling. "Okay. He doesn't give a damn, let's blow it!" cried one of the twins. "All aboard that's going aboard," cried the other. Maria said sweetly, "Pull it now, for the glory of God—His wish is to see the bridge go." April, like me, wanted to go home: "I think we should stop, I don't like it." We all looked at John. "You can't murder a suicide," he said, and pressed the lever on the box he was holding. I stopped loving him at that exact moment, because I had already changed my mind.

The first explosion only rocked the bridge; over by the New York side some heavy cables broke loose and swung down toward the water. The walk started to sway. One of the towers broke in three pieces. Then two more explosions. The bridge cracked. The derelict climbed down from the rail and started to run toward us.

The man who had been bent on suicide now became frantic not to be murdered. I imagine he wanted choice, the choice to be his when and how to die. It may have been that that was all that was left to him when all other pride and control had gradually been stripped away. Or perhaps he had only been playacting, playing with the final solution which he had no intention of taking now—testing his fantasy, but always knowing a safe return was possible. But now the bridge swayed in the wind. The cables frayed and split, and I could see thin wires like a million spider legs jiggling about. I looked down and saw the lights of the bridge sweeping erratically across the dark waters. A piece of tubing fell, splashing, making a circle of white foam. The derelict lost his hat, bent down to pick it up, a beat-up old fedora with the ragged remains of a green feather stuck in the dusty ribbon about the brim. Another blast of dynamite, and the cable broke loose from its top mooring and swung down over the bridge like a high octopus tentacle reaching into the darkness for a victim. A steel rail broke loose and flew into the middle of the bridge, and the derelict tripped over it, screaming "Motherfuckers, help me!" as he fell face forward onto the concrete.

I wanted to be a heroine, to act as my conscience told me, to perform nobly in the highest sense of man's nearness to the angels, but I stood still, my palms wet, my anxiety causing heart palpitations and pains in the chest. I wanted to plunge after him onto the broken bridge, but my feet didn't move because I loved myself and my own life too much for such altruism. Like a pussycat licking her own fur, I intended to make the most of myself.

This was not what he meant at all. John, Maria, April and the twins were already headed for the car. They called to me to come. I waited. I wanted to rush out and get the man, to drag him to my side, but I could hear rumblings, then the sound of thunder on top of me. There were openings on the lower level of the bridge, and the top level cracked apart, flinging the derelict into the Hudson. Intentionally or not, he had reached his tomb.

I was relieved of my indecision. I could not now join John in the car. I desperately wanted to return to my private life but seemed unable to start moving toward a past or a future. Behind me I heard the car start and pull away. John would easily find another woman, and the others had always resented my inclusion in their secret work. I stood watching until a piece of metal tube from a collapsing railing hit me on the hand, crushing my finger. The pain was complete. I cried. My finger was bleeding badly and I became instantly only a brain and a finger. All other interests or considerations fell away as I held my hand and moved rapidly toward help. John had left me because I was only a white, because he was involved in important matters. April would console him for my defection.

I made my way through the gathering crowd of police, local residents, the customers of a nearby diner, and the fire trucks that stood on the Palisades, watching the bridge crumble.

I should have been exhilarated—there were the crowds, unbelieving, excited, just as I had expected, but the derelict bobbing at the bottom of the Hudson, his mouth now full of sewerage and garbage and mud, made the scene less innocent. Blood from my finger dripped onto my brown sandals. I wondered if social action necessarily turned one into Lady Macbeth or if I was just particularly unlucky in this first venture. At last I told a policeman I was hurt. He took me to Englewood's fine hospital where I was adequately taken care of.

After I got home and had slept for many hours, I told Paul I had caught my hand in my friend's Waring blender making a fruit delight. He was so sorry, and he kissed me all over, for which I was very grateful. He told me he would love me whatever the number of fingers I had on my hands. Later, in bed, when I had taken enough medication to stop the acute pain, I thought about the bridge. I was glad we had actually blown it, but I thought again of the derelict and the terror of dying; the nothingness of death swept over me, the small human body, crushed in its free fall—my own bones and blood vessels.

IN WEEK TWO

Today I am back to the routines I know so well. Today they don't seem confining but rather comforting, as if the baby, Elizabeth and Paul, with their ordinary needs, form a shelter over me, and protect me from dangers that without them I would certainly confront. Today as I walked along Broadway, I felt my skirt caught in the hot draft provided by the reverse blow of some huge air conditioner. The heat was curiously pleasing on the top of my thighs and I thought about Paul, the hungry nightly reaching, and all during the day, if I was not otherwise worrying about minor problems, I could feel at odd moments a replay, a memory trace, an additional sensation left over from the night before, appearing in my consciousness as I was throwing the laundry into the washing machine in the basement, or cleaning the baby's ears. (Who is he, that baby? Will he grow to hate me for something I am doing or not doing today?)

Last night Paul and I were talking about revolution. He has become a scholar of disorder and in the course of his studies he has grown more and more convinced that Hobbes's view of man was not black enough. The human animal with its curious uncivil instincts is more evil than even the most hell-fire-damnation-brimstone preacher ever conceived. Each time Judas betrays the revolution and gains power, because he is more ordinary, more like his fellowmen than the best of the idealists who die in prison camps and on guillotines, who die like an echo diminishing to nothing, leaving only the real human voices to bicker and battle, and once again divide the spoils. Paul has told me all this and I report it here, although I don't really choose to believe it. I still think that someday things will change. I don't really believe that there's such a thing as fate. Nothing is written ahead of time in any holy book.

Perhaps Paul was so particularly gloomy last night because he had caught a cold, a curse he felt directly sent by a god whose existence he doubts but whose powers are all too explicit.

This morning he complained of a pain in his chest and a stuffy nose. He decided not to go to the library, but to stay in bed and drink orange juice and brandy—an old college roommate had prescribed this cold cure. I changed the baby, fixed a bottle and put him in a playpen where he might watch his father reading *The New York Times* and admire the Gothic arches on Broadway's other side. If he was attentive, he could see the city pigeons, cooing and messing in the cement folds and on the terraces. I fed Elizabeth her cereal and helped her take off her doll's clothes in preparation for a bath. I made the children's beds and swept a little. I sat down near Paul—his being in bed so long and at this hour gave me a curious sense of joy, of illicit possession. I smoothed his sheets, stirred his brandy with a thermometer, and offered it, germless, to him. He had no fever, only the pale, puffy skin and listless ache that registered a summer cold. The air in the room was hot. There was the ever-present smell in the apartment of diapers, coffee and sweat. He started to complain: the bad timing of his cold, the injustice that he alone should be struck. He sneezed and his eyes turned pink at the rims. It was not fair that now in the middle of his book on "Bloody Revolutionaries, or Idealists Turned Murderers—An Historical Survey" (the title and thousands of notes on index cards were ready) . . . he should not feel well. I walked around the room straightening papers—things in continual disorder I can't really control. Elizabeth appeared wet from her doll's bath. "What'll we do?" She climbed the chairs, she pounced on the pillows, she went into her room and pulled her tea set to the floor. "What'll I do?" she whined. Time, I said, for us all to go out. We left him in bed reading Daniel Defoe's *Journal of the Plague Year* and went out to spend the rest of the morning in the playground.

.   .   .

The oval playground, dirt and clutter—I love its simple way of giving me somewhere to go, something to do that disguises the monotony. How to fill the day—how to get through it?—I can sit on this bench and not feel things are all apart. I am doing what every peasant woman has always done. I am nurturing. Paul sits in the library, in his classroom, and he tries to find some sensible thread, some explanation for bloodshed, revolution, poverty—some design that will close the puzzle and, in adding to our knowledge, add to our redemption—and while he reads and traces similarities and disparities from Plato to Freud, I repeat each day the sameness of everything.

. . .

At night when Broadway is quiet except for the shouts of an occasional drunk, the whine of the ambulance, or the frenetic wail of the police siren—a cry of a child whose night terrors exceed his worst reality—at night when our shade is down and we are in bed together, I am certain that history stands still—that I am not ever to die, and that in the cradling of each other we defy all progress or regression. That illusion always breaks in sleep and the demands of the next day.

The baby reaches from the stroller for a piece of gum paper on the ground. Elizabeth stares at the jungle gym. Its crossbars are now too high for her arm, but soon she'll be able to climb to the top and see the Hudson River, black with pollution flowing out to sea. She'll watch the dayliner plow toward the George Washington Bridge, its passengers already bored with a landscape they must admire for hours more. Now I'll go and hold her on my lap, my child, not yet another person but a limb of mine, struggling like all the other limbs. Maybe later we'll walk down where she can see the river. One Sunday we took the ferry to see the Statue of Liberty. All over the green walls, the offspring of the poor and weary immigrants, grown bold and tasteless like the rest of us, had written in lipsticks and chalk their names, their loves and other obscenities— maybe this desecration is appropriate dress for a lady who promised more than she had to give.

I broke out of my own thoughts for a while and talked to a friend who sat next to me on the bench. We talked about diaper services. Hers seems more efficient than mine. Elizabeth runs laughing to the swing. I will have to chase her to make sure the heavy metal seats don't split her head. I'll buy more ice cream on the way back to the bench.

Soon it will be time to go marketing, to go to the drugstore and buy some nose drops and aspirin, for he will surely have this cold awhile. It will be time for the baby to sleep, and for Elizabeth to lie in her bed sucking on the corner of her blanket. On Broadway I will stop in at the hosiery store and get a pair of black lace pants I've been wanting. When I get home, I mustn't forget to water the geraniums.

. . .

His cold is worse. All through the early hours of the evening he tossed and turned and blew his nose, and I made him hot tea. The heat of the city rose from the streets and brought with it a smell of urine and garbage that invaded our room. Up the side street, even at four in the morning, I could see bodies on the stoops, the sound of Spanish and the radio blending in the heat. The children, too, it seemed, were staying up all night. I could hear their voices, the adults screaming at them and at each other. He talked to me through the dawn of his memories of his home in Massachusetts. He told me of the places he and his brother used to play, of the large fields and the man next door who let the boys ride his horse. He talked like a man who must recall his past before it all fades forever. I suppose the intrusion of germs, however temporary, prompts memory, as if suddenly one were very old and the future empty, and the present bleak, so the mind reconstructs past times to reinforce a sliding sense of being someone. How I wish I could reassure him that all he suffers from is a very bad June cold, and that in a few days he will be back in the library and this episode all forgotten in the flurry of notes and cards and insertions and footnotes that will be taking place.

As I nursed him last night with hot tea and cold compresses, I wondered if he loved me still. I know it's not the same as when he stood on the steps of the Barnard dormitory explaining Eliot's *Four Quartets*. Patiently he went through the poem line by line, and I understood he loved me. Now I just remember it, the way I remember occasionally I have a back or a neck, a spine, a left calf or a right heel. He fell asleep at last when the sky was light gray with the sun approaching slowly across Central Park. I looked at him lying on the rumpled sheets, his shape, his pale face, the bristles of his beard left untended since the cold began, and I wished I could hold him in my arms safe from all disappointments and dangers. I was tired and hot, and I cried, tears from some ready source of grief, because terrible things would surely enter our circle—no wall, no fortress can keep out the gradual erosion of our expectations.

I had just fallen asleep when the baby cried, wet and sticky, hungry and eager to be welcomed. Elizabeth woke a little later, and as I made the breakfast, she played with a puzzle my mother had brought her on her last visit. It had been a fearful visit. Mother had driven in unexpectedly from New Jersey just to see me. When I opened the door and she saw all the toys in the living room I had not yet cleaned up and the dishes in the sink, and the unmade bed, she got very angry, and I sulked as I had years before over similar issues. "I don't even want to put my gloves down anywhere," my mother shrieked, and I felt guilty because she was right, the house was a garbage dump. My mother took the morning *Times* and spread it beneath her on the chair she sat on, a touch I thought not really necessary. As she was leaving, she promised to send me a maid. I should have objected. I was being compromised, but I was too delighted to convincingly refuse the offer. Tomorrow, thank God, the maid comes.

The playground is stifling now, the hot sun on the cement seems to make steam. My friend, who was a year ahead of me at college and whose husband teaches in the Economics Department, has just told me they are expecting a third child. She probably never leaves the beds unmade or the dishes in the sink. I have gone off away from the others so I can write. From this far bench I can see the children—Elizabeth running after a ball, the baby sticking his fingers in the dirt at my friend's feet. The old man with the candy is back. He has carefully taken off his jacket and folded it beneath his cane. He is reading a newspaper and holds in his hand a paper bag which probably contains a doughnut or a pastry he gives himself in the middle of each afternoon. The old lady has returned also. She is sitting near enough to the old man so that a conversation could start—a friendship might form—but so far it hasn't.

The moron is in the playground again. Every day he wanders through the gates. It's hard to tell how old he is, maybe in his teens. His face is flat and his eyes are like slits. His ears are huge and he is very tall and fat around the hips and belly. He walks awkwardly like a small child still not at ease with the skill. He looks indeed like a cartoon monster, and the ladies on the benches turn their eyes away from him—a catastrophe. Thank God, someone else's. His hands hang from his arms open and limp, and saliva drools from the corners of his mouth. It is like seeing a child in an ape's body, man caught at some perilous moment in the evolutionary scale when he can be neither wholly beast nor wholly human. He comes to the playground to be with the little children. The boys chase him in crowds—*bang, bang, bang* go all the guns. "We got you. We got you." Like a brain-damaged Gulliver, he laughs at the Lilliputians, a guttural sound, and runs off. He points his large shapeless fingers back at the attacking crowd. *Bang! Bang! Bang!*—with M-1's, with shields, capguns, water pistols, GI Joe rifles, the group is after him again. He starts to run and stumbles over the edge of the slide. The little boys pull back for a moment frightened, as if they had really gotten the monster and were suddenly uncertain in their purpose. But he gets up again. He has bruised his forehead but he doesn't want to stop the game. *Bang! Bang! Bang!* The little boys follow him behind the water fountain.

He suddenly sees a doll in a doll's carriage being pushed by a pretend-mother. He reaches in and pulls out the doll. He sits down on the ground, sweat pouring off his face, his shirt soaked from the running and the chasing. He holds the doll in his large hands and brings her to his face. Sweetly he starts to lick the doll's face, emitting a kind of soft purring sound. The little girl who was strolling with her carriage starts to cry. Her mother rushes over and, because all of us in the playground are used to the moron, she offers him a pretzel. As he reaches for it, she gently takes the doll and replaces it in the carriage. The moron sits and sucks on his pretzel. The little boys have run off to climb the jungle gym.

Elizabeth is playing with the blue-and-white ball I have just bought her at the five-and-ten on Broadway. It rolls away and I see her chase it and suddenly trip on a toy truck and fall on the cement ground. I am attentive, taut, ready to charge forward. I put down the notebook and in another second I hear her scream as if her universe were empty and her sound would never find a human listener. I run to her and as I get close, I feel her scream in my chest, ready at the edge of an explosion. I see blood pouring from her mouth, covering her chin and staining the pink-and-white flowered dress she's wearing. Quickly I take her in my arms. "Nothing to be frightened of, just a little blood, nothing to worry about—Mommy will fix it." The screaming subsides to a sobbing and my own heart is pounding—so much blood is coming—my arms and the front of my dress are also red. I'm certain it's just a superficial mouth cut, but still my legs are trembling as I carry her to the water fountain. A friend lends me a diaper to use as a towel.—"It's nothing, it's nothing," I say over and over. My life is not my own any more, it belongs in part to her. I have committed myself to taking care of her and I must not fail. She must be the better part of me. She must be the more beautiful, the more graceful, the more loving part of me. I am in and of myself no longer complete, I need her. I wipe with the diaper. I use cold water and press against her pale face and stained mouth, and in a matter of moments she is quiet, leaning on my shoulder. The blood has stopped. Her teeth are all there and I can't even see in her mouth where such a terrible cut could have been. That pink soft tissue opens, profusely bleeds and then closes, leaving no trace of a slash. Elizabeth wants to sit on her seat in the stroller, and now the baby who has watched the drama with open eyes wants to be held and smiled at. I give them both cookies and sit back on the bench, the baby on my lap. The heat again fools like a weight, like someone stuffing cotton down one's chest. Sometimes as I sit watching the children I suddenly think of Paul, of the smell and feel of him. I don't know if the images I have are lascivious or tender, I think perhaps they are both. In and out of my mind all during the day move thoughts of him.

Paul's sleeping now on our bed, breathing heavily, his hair wet across his forehead. Not tonight, tonight I'll be too tired, he won't be well enough, but certainly tomorrow or perhaps in the early morning he'll reach over and touch my breasts and I'll roll toward him and for a while nothing else will matter, not his cold, not our children, not the book on revolutions—it will all wait for us to finish, to separate again.

The baby is struggling to move around. I put him down off my lap and take from his hand a cigarette about to go into his mouth. I watch as he crawls to the next bench, and quickly I jump up and grab him before his fingers get caught beneath a carriage wheel. I put him back in the stroller and he cries in fury. His face turns red, his period of freedom was too short, too delicious, to be given up so quickly. But I'm tired, I cannot watch him, protect him with total vigilance, and one accident a day is enough. The other mothers are looking at me. Why is that child screaming, why doesn't she do something? She's probably one of those cold, indifferent types, the kind that breed damaged children; hasn't she read Bettelheim, Spock, Gesell? I give him a smile, I push the stroller back and forth. Elizabeth leans forward and tickles his cheek—which usually makes him laugh. Nothing works. Elizabeth pinches him too hard, the pinch of anger, at his tears, at his very existence. He cries louder. I am an interfering, spoiling mother and from the sound of his crying I am never to be forgiven. From the strength of her pinch I can tell she will never forgive me for having borne him. It's early but I'm going to leave this hot playground and go to the air-conditioned pizza place on 115th Street. The children will cover themselves with tomato sauce. I will sit in the dark booth, my elbows on the shiny Formica tabletop, and play the jukebox. And then at last it will be time to go home.

I was thinking about Paul's cold earlier today. I noticed how pale and mottled his face was and the sticky damp dark spots on the sheets, and the frail sound of his nasal voice humming Mozart melodies as he watched the afternoon's soap opera on television—What when he is really ill, what when he or I lie in bed dying? It is absolutely certain that one of us will die before the other, and the stronger one will tend the sick one, grow to loathe the illness and the patient, and then suddenly be left alone, like a statue without arms, legs or nose, be permanently undone. That thought can't be tolerated long and yet it can't be pushed entirely aside, because the moment will arrive and I want my perceptions and attitudes to be ready, I want to be prepared.

Once last March Elizabeth ran a fever of 104 and her breath came heavy, slow and painful. The doctor came, not very disturbed, and used penicillin. A sharp disposable needle, a cry from Elizabeth, a pat on my back, a prescription on the table, and he was gone. I stayed up all that night, bringing her cold washcloths, rubbing her chest with alcohol, watching the vaporizer and the strange shapes that appeared in the steam. I wasn't really frightened, but as I stared at her flushed face and the dilated pupils, I realized that I couldn't be without her—that I had fiercely and passionately involved myself in the limbs and brain, the body and soul of my child. Why? Why was I proud when she learned numbers early, pleased when she fitted together pieces of a puzzle, proving an intelligence expected and necessary for survival? Why was I embarrassed when she wet her pants in the playground and the urine streamed down her legs, settling in puddles in her socks—why was I so angry and hurt the day the little boy called her "Cross-eyes" and wouldn't play daddy in her game of house? Why did I nearly cry as I held her in my arms and explained that he was just a bad boy? Is it something perhaps in the secret sticky protoplasm out of which I molded her— myself now devoted to a replica of myself, now slave, now master, caught in a bind; not pleasant, certainly *nowhere* happy, predictably bound for clashing of wills, disappointments, expectations unmet, pride hurt—all that I know will happen between a mother and a daughter, between me and Elizabeth. What do I want from her when she grows up? Whatever it is, I am sure I won't get it. Whatever she will do will be less than what I have planned, because I can't help planning so much, asking so much of her. I always used to share the joke and point the finger at the ambitious stage mother, or the possessive Jewish mother whose son could not go to the bathroom without her following behind to wipe and admire his parts. And now I think those are visible caricatures of the even more sinister reality, the more ordinary poisonous ooze that flows between parent and child—Elizabeth is marred because she is mine and each waking hour I transmit in a thousand unconscious ways the necessary code for her to absorb my personality, to identify with my sex, and to catch, like a communicable plague, all my inadequacies and mimic them or convert them to massive ugly splotches on her own still young soul. For example, I have never told her in any kind of words that I am afraid of the dark, and yet she will not let me put out her bedside lamp and I don't insist, because I remember giants and witches, evil blobs of unknown menace, lying directly at the cover's edge when it's dark. I still sometimes feel an unseen presence behind my back, readying itself to leap and force me into some unspeakable violence. Sometimes I think perhaps it's wrong, morally wrong, to have children, when I am so uncertain whether or not I am a good person, enough of a person to create another. I so badly want my children to grow strong and be meaningfully rebellious, to take some corner of the earth and claim it for their own. I look around me in the playground at all the other mothers and their children. We are united in our strong feelings of ambition for our children.

Elizabeth is sometimes afraid of dogs, large ones that pull on their leashes or little ones that bark too much. Sometimes she's afraid of the moon. She says it's like a ghost hand in the sky. Sometimes she curls up in my lap and says she wishes she were the tiny baby in the house, that growing up is a nasty thing. I point out all the wonders of maturity, but I still can't convince her. Sometimes she seems to want to contract until she's no more than a few cells, visible only through a microscope, nestling against the wall of my sealed-off uterus. I too sometimes would like to progress in reverse so my mother could brush my hair each morning and complain about my roller skates left out to rust in the backyard, so I could take my dolls to bed and draw pictures in my schoolbooks of a prince waiting to make me, Margaret Ferguson of Paramus, New Jersey, his bride.

How was I before Elizabeth was born? Even though it's only a few short years, I seem to have always listened for the sound of a child's crying or calling. When I think of losing her, and of illness, long nights in the hushed corridors of bleak hospitals, the sound of children crying for their mothers or their teddy bears, and nurses rustling by in the dark whispering bad news to each other, I think about how I would drink dark coffee out of paper cups, and wait. Sometimes I am frightened of a possible car crash, a fall, a pot of boiling water overturned, a bobbypin experimentally poked into an electric socket. And then, after the death, I would be a woman with a limb amputated—worse, perhaps, I would be a woman with a hole in the center, in the bowels, a great gaping hole from breast to genitals, for the wind to blow through, for trash to collect in, for everyone to know I am emptied of myself.

I must pick up Elizabeth from the dirt by the water fountain where she is sitting with another little girl, drawing in the mud. There is a leak at the base of the fountain and it has created a miniature river whose geography is being carefully studied by the children. She is dirty, and I like to see her that way. The dirt is from the feeling and the touching of all possible surfaces, and a certain lack of concern, a certain pleasure in doing things uninhibited by prissy thoughts and stuffy manners. The baby is sleeping on his back, his hands flung out on either side of the stroller. Too late for pizza, instead I will take them both home and stop at the drugstore and pick up some cough medicine for Paul. Maybe if I can find enough change hidden in the corners of my bag, I can bring him the *New American Review* to take his mind off his nasal congestion.

OUT OF WEEK TWO

Last week the editor of the Columbia *Forum* called and asked me to do an article on women in Cuba. I immediately contacted *Look* Magazine and made an agreeable arrangement with them. I spoke to my mother and she consented to take the children for several weeks until I finished the assignment. Paul will have to manage. He can eat dinner at the West End Bar and make himself coffee for breakfast. Of course I don't like leaving him, my familiar love, the weather of my life, but the climate of opinion and my own opinion is that a female must follow her own inclinations. Staring at your man too long and too intently can turn a woman into a pillar of salt, to be abandoned in the general flight to greener lands. I won't be a salt brick to be licked by any passing bovine with a thick sandpaper tongue.

I know Paul has experiences away from me that he keeps private, uses to enrich himself. His mind; his soul is only partially the sum of our united life. I want the same separateness. I want to grow strong and older with more than age. I want to learn something myself.

So I packed my few summer dresses, my trenchcoat in case it rained, and bought myself at Bloomingdale's large wide dark glasses. Like a bulletproof vest or a knight's silver armor, they will protect me from all unwanted penetration from the outside.

On the plane to Mexico to make connections to Cuba, I remembered all the things I had heard about Havana before the Revolution: the ladies of the night who made it with donkeys on nightclub floors to the wild amusement of sailors on wartime leave; the gambling tables, the luxurious hotels; the women plump and eager—for sale—almost all of them for sale for a minimal price—the very rich in jewels and Paris-designed gowns, and the poor hanging around, their faces aging by the second, until like unharvested grapes, they bruised, rotted and dropped back into the soil. I had heard that Havana, now in the height of revolutionary ardor, was very dull, like a whore turned nun.

But I had a romance of revolution in my head, a radical prayer that envisioned not lines of men with ration books and new buildings that looked like army barracks, but scythes swinging in rhythmic unison on fields of wheat, children singing songs of a new future, dropping flowers on the graves of dead heroes. I wanted to believe that greed, exploitation, hopelessness, religious excess, could all be put to sleep by the people working together. Idealist, romanticist that I cannot help but be, I looked forward to visiting Cuba to see for myself the world created anew.

I drank in the bar that first night with other newsmen, a Czech sociologist and an Albanian linguist. I heard some stories that I may be able to use in my article, one that particularly interested me.

. . .

In a far village, the appointed leader, Carlos, was a respected, shrewd and handsome peasant whose broad shoulders and flashing eyes (my poster peasant) demanded respect from all who lived under his domination. One summer a host of university students descended on the village to help with the gathering of the cane. They slept on the local schoolhouse floor and were fed by the local people, an equal share in all their food. One young girl among them found the work particularly hard, and each day in the sun she would feel faint and have to lie down against the dark soil and wait for strength to return to her limbs. She was a chemistry student; her mother had been a ballet dancer and her father a librarian. She herself hoped in the new Cuba to be a doctor, but her stamina was not great, and her body was so delicate, her wrist bones so small, she looked like a ballet dancer Carlos had once seen in a picture magazine. He started to aid her with her chores, to assign her simple easy tasks and to sit by her side as she cleaned the vegetables with inept fingers unused to such ordinary labor. His wife was spread fat from eating too much, from eight childbearings and from a peasant ancestry of wide-ankled heavy-armed women who could carry on their heads the wash of a week and on their backs the children, piles of children like stones hewed from the quarry and brought to the house to build the walls. His wife watched as he took the young girl gently into the fields and carried her back in his arms late at night to her bed in the communal dormitory. His wife narrowed her eyes to slits when later he returned to his conjugal bed and merely pushed her aside to make more room for his already relaxed body.

Like the rage that broke down the doors of the Bastille, jealousy boiled inside her until the next week she denounced him to central headquarters in Havana, claiming that he had told her of plans to keep from the village store a large share of food and goods for his own family, and ultimately to escape by a small fishing boat to Miami. Carlos was removed from the village and sent to hard labor in a far part of the country. After the scandal had died down, Carlos' wife recovered from her shock and proposed that she herself become leader of the village, and those in power in Havana thought this an appropriate reward for her revolutionary loyalty and vigor. She ran the village so well, she commanded such respect from all her workers that the obscure area became a model which was visited by dignitaries from countries all over the world.

After a year or so, she missed her husband and requested of the Central Committee that he be returned to her. They were hesitant to free a subversive, a reactionary of such bad character, and only when she agreed to hold him under house arrest, which—since there was no extra personnel to guard him— meant keeping him chained to the bed most of the time, did they agree to release him in her custody. And so it is that deep in the provinces a wasted man can be found manacled to his bed, waiting the nightly attentions of his busy but triumphant wife.

The story got around as such stories will, and did more to keep men faithful to their spouses than had centuries of indoctrination by the local priests. It seems in this country politics can become a cosmetic to disguise a woman's fading charms and keep her desirable to the man of her choice.

As we sat in the bar of the once elegant hotel eating peanuts from little ashtrays, faces blurred in the rosy fluorescent lighting, a strange comradeship developed among us—reporters, journalists, strangers to the town we visited—a protective sense, a friendship for one another, an illusion of safety in group love—a beautiful high caused by the distance from home and familiar relationships, and the closeness to any near body that was willing to lean and be leaned on. We talked of politics and wars, general subjects that still reveal very quickly the intimate person. I found myself on a worn bar stool next to the Albanian linguist; he created an interesting word connection. The name Castro meant, he thought possibly, in the old Latin as adopted by the Church, both camp, as in military use, and one of the castrated, one whose body has been altered to assure him of a sweet voice in the choir. I told him that in America the word had become synonymous with a kind of sofa that converted at night to a bed. "Very American," he answered me with a disapproving shake of his head. "To cast is also an expression used in fishing," I said, anxious to remedy any bad materialistic impression I might have made. "The line is thrown out to as correct a point as possible above the head of the swimming fish. We also speak of castaways as lost persons, people thrown out, never reeled in like the fishing line. A cast is also something in which we encase a broken limb, made of plaster and such." The Albanian wrote down everything I said in a notebook. He was attractive enough, a little pale, with eyes so bleached out that one could almost see through to the tissues and veins protecting his brain cells.

Whenever I think of Albania, images come to mind of savage Turks sweeping down on little villages, peasants cowering behind haystacks, bodies lying beside dead horses on the roadside, or again, of Nazi tanks plowing through fields of daisies while the local priest huddles around him in a white church on a hill women and children uselessly praying. Albanians are victims of a history they can neither create nor avoid. Like the existence of sand crabs and minnows, their survival seems itself a wonder. As I looked at this very well-educated man, I realized I had forgotten in my image of Albania the landed nobility whose offspring would study in Bucharest or Paris, and whose childhood would be overrun with Russian tutors and French dancing teachers. But these images jarred against the political revolutionary talk around us. Besides being a very religious Communist, my companion, I soon learned, had a rather ordinary lust for Western women, whose style he had admired in Paris, Prague and Vienna, where his studies had often taken him.

He soon enough asked me to continue our interesting derivations in his room, quoting some statement of Mao's on love as the twelfth path to victory. I don't like to consider myself bourgeois, middle-class, or sexually unresponsive. However, I wasn't entirely sure I found his pale eyes at all appealing—but then there is the matter of sleeping alone: the bed is cold and there seems to be something perverse in single sleep. I went with him. He had white, thin hair over his whole body, like peach fuzz, and happily I discovered that I was particularly fond of the soap they used in his country, a soap made of beeswax and cow dung; its aroma, like nothing I had ever before smelled, lent an exotic air to this otherwise probably unexceptional encounter.

I love to be loved, to be admired, to have a new man approve; promiscuity or just reasonable reassurance?—I'm not sure. Alone I wonder if I measure up. I know I'm not a *Vogue* model or an actress or a teenager in a miniskirt. I brood about all the obvious unfavorable comparisons. I wonder if I'm good enough, brain and body aging in a complicated way. But with a man, an uncommitted man with whom there has not been time for balances of payments to collect, credits and debits to hang about the neck—with a new man I am again Venus on her shell, rising lightly to the surface of the ocean, beautiful, pure, coming in to shore composed and happy.

I don't think it's nice to keep lists of sexual exploits, like notches on a gunbelt, or black books with names and telephone numbers. I once went on an assignment with a photographer who said that his greatest fear was that one day he would walk into a restaurant or a party, and be greeted by a past amour, and have no memory of having taken her. It was of course his hope that this would happen—it would mean his exploits had reached into numbers beyond counting or remembering. I plan to look totally blank when next I meet him. But I do confess I'd like to have a secret place where I could put up the flags of all the nationalities with which I have been intimate, a kind of sexual United Nations, illustrating that language, race and color are no barriers to pleasure.

The Albanian had a long tongue like an anteater and he coated it with vodka frequently. I wonder if it was some sort of physiological adaptation to profession that made his tongue so extensive and explorative.

The next morning I interviewed the female chief of the Havana Main Hospital, Dr. Maria Lopez. She was married to an economist on the University staff and had a child, she told me confidentially. She seemed an excellent example of the new Cuban woman. She clearly enjoyed her work, which included administrative control over a large number of new buildings. She complained, as everyone in Havana complains, of shortages. She needed more proper X-ray machines, heart respiratory pumps, tools of all kinds, laboratory equipment, medicines. Still she was enormously proud of the accomplishments and skills of her staff. She herself delivered babies from time to time, her original specialty. Her breasts were huge, her hips wide, and something in her walk reminded me of the old Havana, of those legendary ladies of the night whose trade was not learned at the University. She seemed an ideal combination of things sexual and intellectual.

"Dr. Lopez," I asked, "have you anything to say to the women of America?"

And suddenly this simple question elicited an explosive and emotional response, not at all the political speech I had expected.

"Give," she said. "Give generously, from your golden streets and your golden pocketbooks. You are the hope of the world. You are so powerful and rich. Give for research, give to discover the cause and cure of mental retardation." She sounded suddenly like the pitchwomen at various luncheons I had attended with my mother. But more than that, an edge in her voice told me she was desperate for help, help for herself.

"Why," I asked, "are you so passionate in particular about this disease? So many illnesses remain incurable. Is this a particularly serious problem in Cuba?" I pressed her.

"But this one," she said, "is different. There is no disaster more heartbreaking; more families are destroyed by the diseased brain of a newborn—more pain and waste are caused by this terrible plague which leaves children blanketed in darkness, sucking their thumbs, rocking on their haunches, unable to achieve the simplest of satisfactions yet able still to feel all the ache of rejection and the loneliness of abandonment. The damage affects a child's abilities, but it leaves him with the emotional capacity to carry on, concealed from the world's eye; lonely and scared like you and me, they wait, these children, like miners trapped underground by an explosion, for the fumes of their environment to overcome them, releasing them to an early death.

This disease I know well, because it affects my own son. I look at him rocking back and forth with his hands waving before his face and his eyes slanted without sparkle or any kind of reflection—a near vegetable, a maimed animal, a creature beyond help, and I am in grief greater than can be imagined. Tell the women in America. They are rich. Give money, give money. America must finally cure everything with its money."

This last she confided in a whisper. Clearly it was an indiscreet thought for a pioneer in a brave new socialist nation. I felt an unjust disappointment in her. I had wanted her to be cool and rational, like the chief surgeons in New York hospitals—to stand at some astronomical distance from the species and operate, manipulate, ameliorate when possible, but Dr. Lopez was not that. She was simply a mother who was hurt. A doctor, an administrator—all these facets of her accomplishments did not protect her from crucifixion on the cross of motherhood.

"But, Dr. Lopez," I said, "you are fortunate to have such a full professional life that you are much more than the mother of a damaged child."

She looked at me coldly and said in a bitter tone, "You are an American. You cannot understand what family is, what mother is. When I learned, when I knew for sure that my baby would be dumb, alone with strange thoughts in the thick folds of his misshapen brain, I felt as if all my limbs had been cut off, as if I could no longer move about my world because the pain would destroy us both." I made allowances for tropical temperament, but I moved away from her toward the window as one moves away from any disaster that comes too threateningly close. "You are young. I have scared you." She came behind and put her arm around my shoulder. "Don't be alarmed," she said. "I am only a woman protesting despite the scientist in me, protesting the errors of nature—wanting the miracle of life to be each time perfect, not as it is sometimes, on one side or the other of beauty."

"Dr. Lopez," I said, embarrassed, "do you think the women in Cuba have improved their lot since the revolution? That's the subject of my article, the subject of my research."

"Of course," she said, warm and inviting. "Have you not spoken to Fidel, El Capitan?"

"No," I replied. "I haven't been able to arrange an interview. Since the subject of my article is women, I had not thought to press for it."

"Well, come tonight then, my little American," she said, "to our house for dinner, and you will meet the great one himself, and you can discuss women's role with him. It is absolutely one of his favorite subjects, and I know he would want to talk to you about it. You may bring a male friend if you like, but absolutely no photographers. It is a private dinner, for social, not socialist, purposes."

That was how my Albanian linguist and I found ourselves

at the home of the Doctors Lopez, meeting, eating, talking intimately with El Capitan himself. My first impression of the man later proved correct: something soft in the face, odd in the movements, and a voice hoarse, scratchy, higher pitched than one would have expected, but just as electric. All night delicious food was served by maids in starched uniforms. Just as in capitalist countries, someone must do the dishes and mop up the floor. What happens when they are all educated for better things is that all women become slaves again. Fidel moved, his two bodyguards at his side, among the guests, talking of communal harvests, factory output and university expansion. Like all men whose work has absorbed their souls, he conversed only on his own concerns. I saw my Albanian linguist in deep conversation with two young ladies from Peking. I stayed with them long enough to find out that one's mission in Cuba was to sell a cookbook called *Chinese Cooking Made Easy* that she herself had translated into eight languages. Her comrade, whose Spanish was less adequate than hers, told me through the Albanian interpreter that she was attempting to arrange an import deal whereby the Cubans, in return for several captured American planes, would receive five hundred laundry wash-and-dry machines just manufactured by a new factory outside of Fuchou.

I watched Fidel move among the guests in his baggy khakis and field jacket. His motions were odd, like those of a kangaroo or a giraffe, as if the clothes were too big and as if he were alert for danger at each moment, watching everyone from the corners of eyes that moved restlessly about the room. An uncommon man, a genius. I could see that in his eyes. The bushy unkempt hair seemed to hide a certain softness around the mouth; his teeth were startlingly small. If his world had been different, I would have bet that he would have become a poet or a painter.

I finally made my way to the great man's side. He seemed pleased to meet me. I told him my assignment and was rewarded with considerably more than an account of the official political position on women. Of course, that too. He talked for hours on education, community nursery schools, easy abortion, equality of opportunity, instant divorce, and all the things that everyone all over agrees must be done if women are to fulfill their social and personal potential. He told me that he had decorated two female factory foremen just that day, but there was something much more he revealed, not for publication in the Columbia *Forum* or in *Look* Magazine.

"Why do you think," he said to me, "that there has never been a great woman mathematician or composer? A performer or two, yes, but no composers or conductors. Why?" he asked, his eyes sad.

"I don't know," I said, trying not to sound irritated. "Men have asked me that question over and over for the last ten years. Perhaps because women don't care to arrange and rearrange abstract relationships; they are busy with human matters," I answered him, not paying too much attention to my own words.

"Nonsense," he roared, and the fanatic's luminosity burned in his eyes. "It has to do with progression. Before math and music there must be politics, female presidents, heads of state, not like the English queen, but elected, revered, female commando heroes."

Somehow his fervor on that subject made me smile.

"It's been years since the women got the vote in America," I reminded him, "and there have been more wars, depressions, and social disasters since that date than before it." I was flirting in my own way.

"What the world needs," he said, "is not a Joan of Arc, the kind of woman who allows herself to be burned on the cross. That's just a bourgeois invention meant to frighten little girls into staying home. What we require is a real female military social leader."

"But that"—I smiled at him—"is just impossible. Women are tied to husband and children. Women are constructed to be penetrated; a sword or a gun in their hands is a joke or a mistake. They are open holes in which things are poured. Occasionally, it's true, a woman can become a volcano, but that's about it."

He laughed, he liked me, and he wanted to confide in me, to tell me the truth, a truth that no one would believe if I should be so indiscreet as to spread it around. That's why, I suppose, he was not afraid to tell me.

After the other members of the party had gone home, Fidel asked me if I would go with him for the night. My Albanian was following me around with a hangdog look. I sent him back to the hotel with an empty promise of a late night rendezvous.

At the simple house where Castro lived, there was no pomp or ceremony. In fact, there were dirty dishes in the sink, cigar ashes everywhere, books, articles, back issues of *Pravda* and *The New York Times* scattered across the floor, with an article or two of clothing I presumed to be dirty laundry; coffee cups and a silver-framed picture of his mother rested underneath the piano. It was a true bachelor's pad. We had a drink or two. I looked at the photographs of army comrades, village schools and factories that were tacked all over the walls. I admired the llama rug that had been sent by some revolutionaries who were passing through Peru. At last he dismissed the body-guards and pulled the blinds. I thought it was the beginning of the usual seduction scene and I curled up on his sofa, already planning on my indispensable role to our State Department.

A woman can have power if she sleeps with a man who holds it, of course. It is indeed transferable through the semen, through the sexual touch—and it is true that power is as appealing a lure for ladies as youth, wealth, intelligence, and all the other obvious attractions. I was sitting near to Fidel, excited by my approaching contact with the head of state, an ordinary American girl from the suburbs of New Jersey, with only an A-minus in a few history papers to qualify me for a role in political events. I was also frightened. Would I die in his fire like Eva Braun, would I be pulverized in his enormous heat, would I remember to go home in time to Paul and Elizabeth and the baby?

He asked me to close my eyes for a moment and he would tell me when to open them. I did it like a child expecting a birthday surprise, like a woman expecting a welcome sexual attack. It's happened to me before, and I waited, patiently, in the dark. After a long while he asked me to look and I opened my eyes. His face was directly next to mine, but there was no beard, no sign of a beard, no stubble from a recent shave—just smooth soft skin, a gentle jaw. And his bushy eyebrows were gone, in their place, sloping arches of thin hair. I nearly screamed. Then like a rabbit in a headlight's glare, I tensed my body for a flight that never came. He stood up and took off his khaki army shirt, revealing baggy underwear with a hole in it. He took that off too, and I saw on his chest two breasts, round, full, with nipples extending erect from the sudden cold

air . . . a heavy chest, fat folds—not every man has hair on
his chest, sometimes a tropical disease can make it all fall out,
I tried to tell myself, but I knew I was seeing breasts, the kind
that carry milk glands, sexual nerve endings, and occasionally
fatal tumors. In other words, the kind of breasts I myself
possessed. He took off his belt and dropped his fatigues to the
floor and then the underpants, and I saw a mound with pubic
hair curled, and a slit, and he sat down naked except for socks
that wrinkled about the ankles and the heavy black boots. His
gunbelt hung on a nearby chair, and a carbine rested on the
desk. He sat down and spread his legs—unshaved legs, but in
shape unmistakably female. I saw a woman, a heavy, not
beautiful, muscular and awkward woman. Physiologically,
anatomically, absolutely, I saw a woman. I was as frightened
as if I had seen, instead of genitals just like my own, a
Frankenstein monster, a vampire, a ghost from a childhood
terror.

"Don't come any closer," I yelled, wishing I carried a
weapon, a bottle of Mace in my purse, a fountain pen that shot
bullets, some little protection for a lady in a tight spot. It was
a nightmare—time to wake up—time for him to transform
back. Oh, Wizard of Oz, I want to go back to Kansas . . . I
nearly cried.

He laughed. "I use electronics, mikes, amplifiers, to keep
my voice deep, and for the rest, it's a simple disguise, the kind
that you can buy in any large city in America. At the end of
my next five-year plan, I will reveal the secret to the country,
and then women will go dancing in the streets, and they will
rush to their desks, capable at last of higher mathematics and
musical composition, revolutionary leadership and all the
things that make manifest true equality between the sexes, and

then, and only then, will the total revolution have been achieved, the revolution of women against their oppressors —men."

He had come closer on the couch and took my hand. "I am sad, you know," he said. "My secret requires that I live alone and only occasionally come close to the body of another. But I am doing this for all of Cuba and all of womankind, whose reflections on themselves will never be the same again after I reveal myself as a truly female leader." He turned out the light, kicked his boots away, and unzipped my dress. I loved him for his enormous power, his great sacrifice of personal happiness and for his body—just like mine.

Later he dressed, pasted back on the beard and the eyebrows. I was shocked, and incredulous. The events of the evening had bewildered me as when many many years ago the little boy down the block had told me what parents do together to conceive children. Unbelievable, a fantastic assault on the ordinary imagination—that people behind doors without clothes should actually behave in that peculiar way and that I myself would do the same. Things that are inconceivable in the lobbies of movie houses or crowded living rooms could be done in the privacy of bedrooms. I had looked at the naked Castro and I had told him I loved him— But soon he thought of history again and called for his driver to take me back to my hotel.

I found the Albanian pacing about before my door, but for once I didn't want anything but obliterating, unconfusing, single sleep.

I told Paul about Castro's true genitals when, after collecting interviews with farm women, factory workers and shopgirls, I returned home. He thought I was joking, and

nothing, not my tears, my sullen withdrawal, my deep pro-
testations, nothing would convince him I was not playing
about with serious matters, turning history (absurd, maybe,
but nevertheless sacrosanct) into dirty psychosexual drama.
And so I decided to try to forget the entire experience. But
secretly I knew that part of me would remain forever faithful
to Fidel.

IN WEEK THREE

Today is the first Monday morning in July, and Paul is over his cold and back in the library. I sit in the playground and watch Elizabeth running in and out of the sprinkler the Park Commissioner has at last turned on. She wears a little bathing suit with ruffles my mother brought for her on Sunday. She fills her pail with water and then spills it on her toes. Sometimes she throws it on Liza, her friend in water play. It's hard to sit here and not envy the children's unbelievable pleasure in the stream of water and their sense of joy and power when they throw a towel over the fountain head, stopping the supply, and then pull back the towel, screaming as the water with additional force spurts up toward the sun. I sit here separated from the other mothers by my own need for privacy. I am either a hypochondriac or a realist, depending on your point of view. This morning, after I had fed the baby and was lying back under the sheets, with Paul still sleeping, his body all over on my side of the bed—he always slides over, his arms and legs searching for mine when I slip out to answer a child's cry—this morning I decided to check my breasts for lumps, swellings or unusual dimplings—my breasts that caused me such anguish by growing too soon and making me conspicuous in the fifth grade at Paramus Junior High—the same breasts that give me such pleasure when Paul touches them with his hands, or even just his eyes. I felt about them clinically. I couldn't stop myself from thinking about the time when I will find something, the time when I will be routinely squeezing and will bump against something hard, and an alarm will go through my whole body. At the point of discovery, of course, it will be too late. I try to stop the direction of my thoughts but am overwhelmed. I see it all, the surgery, the scars, the brave way I will carry my body, less than what it was, but not yet defeated—and then the final coma, the funeral, and Paul looking about his freshman class, searching in the stacks of the library, for a replacement. Now that he is older and more experienced, he may even choose better, a neater, more precise kind, a mathematician or a biophysicist with contact lenses that do not irritate her eyelids and are never left on sink tops or in laundry baskets. I think of Elizabeth and the baby without me, and I feel the sense of their loss. Their intimate knowledge of death sweeps over me, causing me to wake Paul, and cry on his neck and rub his chest and demand to be petted till the nightmare–daydream retreats before his determined erection and our early morning lovemaking.

Is it hypochondriacal to think often of the final disease, the one that's going to get you? Don't soldiers think of the bullet, the one with their name on it, that might puncture a lung, a heart or vital stomach tissue? It seems natural to think of death when the body is so clearly a pregnable frame, when it's so simple to sever life—a clog in the heart, a spill of blood in the brain, a malignant invasion, bacteria or carcinoma, a lung with fluid, a stomach with a bleeding sore, a liver shriveled like a prune, sending poisons back into the arteries—an aberrant blood cell digesting its neighbor, a colon that collapses. I am certain these are not things to dwell on—just go to the doctor for yearly checkups, Pap smears and chest thumpings . . . And still I sit on the bench in the playground remembering, reconstructing the visions of my vulnerability that reappear at odd moments throughout the day. Unlike Joan of Arc's voices, they don't encourage any action, aggressive or defensive, but they do leave me—typical of a mystical trance—absorbed by the productions of my own brain. I wish I knew nothing of my own biological fate, but like a plant could flower in my season, shed a seed to an indifferent wind, contract to dust without a moment's regret or anticipation. It's the anticipation that's probably the most difficult part.

The secret is denial, pretense. Everyone else on the block will get polio this summer, but of course I will be spared. Never give it another thought. The boy in the eighth grade is in the hospital with rheumatic fever—never will happen to me. The sexy teenage sister of my best friend has spilt her guts all over the Jersey Turnpike at two in the morning—a wage of sin; nothing like that will happen to me. I'm like a city horse with blinders on so he won't see the cars nearly clip off his legs; a little denial helps. I would be grateful just to see the narrow road ahead, even if the path led straight to the glue factory. If only there were some talisman, some magic gesture, some holy water I could sprinkle, some garlic to wear around my neck. If only I could convince myself the Angel of the Lord, recognizing hidden virtues, has smeared the lamb's blood on my doorfront, and my family will be exempt from plagues of every conceivable variety.

When I was a child, naturally I loved the swimming pool with its turquoise water, its shimmering lights, and I always found it hard to believe that it, such a source of pleasure, should be a breeding place for deadly germs. My mother always warned me to keep my mouth closed—at least one plugged-up orifice was better than none. Did it or did it really not cut down on the possibility of serious infection? Was it due to this caution that I was spared?

The baby, now thirteen months, stands in the stroller, kicks at its sides. Soon I will give in to his justified irritation and let him crawl under the sprinkler, soaking his diaper, crawling on the muddy cement, let him run on his sturdy plump legs, rushing about to take what toys other children have left unguarded. Will I smother him with mother love and tie him to me with an Oedipal rope? Naturally all the women's magazines, and an occasional best seller, caution against too much love, too much stimulation, sex where modesty should be, and I will honestly try not to be seductive, never to flirt inappropriately. I promise to remind myself, hands off—eyes off—thoughts off—that small sweet penis that alternately smells of urine, b.m., powder, baby lotion and diaper rash preventives—zinc oxide, Vaseline, Ivory soap—and for this little while is confided to my exclusive care.

I'm a few days late for my period—doesn't even need thinking about. Sometimes I'm a few days early, sometimes a few days late. I'm not a clock or a machine with interlocking parts moving in dependable rhythms. I have an erratic brain pattern, and no doubt an individual menstrual whim. But nevertheless with each passing hour I begin to build an unannounced, semiconscious anticipation. Could it possibly be that cell one is hooking on to the uterine wall, cells eight, identical DNA, RNA patterns, sending signals, digesting, puffing and dividing? Cells sixteen: cervix closed, pinker, a liquid sac, no more than a drop or two of water protecting the sixteen cells. Not sixteen—thirty-two DNA patterns, potential brain waves or sex organs. Sixty-four cells under the ordinary flesh of my stomach, muscles still not back to where they were when I was mooning over the lifeguard on the Jersey shore, that first summer I petted in the back seat of a car; a hundred and twenty-eight cells, a blob, an entity, acids, proteins, protoplasm, helix, double, quadruple. I sit here on the bench in the hot July sun. I am not moving a limb, almost as if I'm hoping that if I am quiet enough, I will hear or feel a growing, dividing tiny fetus that may be my next baby. Of course this is nonsense. What is actually happening is that an egg, unmet by X or Y sperm, has waited its time out, even perhaps hung in the upper regions of the moist dark womb a little longer, unwilling to drop, but now—like an old lady, whose disheveled hair and waving thin arms and stockings slipping down stick legs reveal through lack of firm lines and distinct form her coming death—just so the edges of my egg are stretched out, fraying, and the nucleus once so bright with expectation is fogged over with chemical dissolution, and it slips, my egg, down toward the bottom of the womb, and the tissues of the walls, once so hospitable, now shed and tear themselves down, engulfing the protons and neutrons and molecules, remains of egg, and soon the downward push will enter the vaginal cavity and ooze out between my legs—waste product like urine and feces, like a snake's last year's skin, like clipped toenails in the toilet bowl. Unnecessary for survival, a part can be rejected without any grief. On the other hand, as I sit here I think to myself perhaps there are two hundred and forty-eight cells beginning to make a shape, outlines of a head, bent over what seems to be small knees curled up.

Paul would find another baby quite intolerable. Last night he was explaining to me how strange it seemed to him to be a father at all, even to be teaching, to be handing out grades and lecturing to faces raised up to him. Such a short while ago, just yesterday, it seems, he was an ordinary bright student, a young man with a passionate conviction that our society was immoral and in need of change. A siege of TB had made him ineligible for the draft and so he was spared the agonizing tests of values involved in that, and then he had a father, a man who sent money and letters admonishing his son to follow his true bent, to avoid the wicked traps of the city, to come back to the Berkshires and work on his father's newspaper and go fishing in the clear lakes of his boyhood. But then, he says, it seems as if his life speeded up, as if the camera went doubletime, and he met me and we raced along Broadway and Riverside Drive, arms about each other, as if no two other people had ever felt or known the sweet connection, the final refuge we found in each other's company. We kissed on street corners and laughed too loud on buses; we exhibited, wanted everyone to see, that we were special, exempt from the loveless, empty disasters we saw around us. Then it seemed to him as if we galloped, as in old Marx Brothers movies, and tumbled to the Justice of the Peace, and without his being at all clear on its implications, he found himself my husband, an instructor of history in the School of General Studies, and a doctoral candidate, with a working wife, an apartment, a hi-fi set, dishes that matched from my mother, carpeting of sorts, a modern sofa—a gift from my aunt—and there he was, the owner of objects, of books. All he lacked now, he grumbled, was the life insurance policy that his father with all his Yankee caution was forever pressing him about. The children came so fast, he complained—he had had to change from son to father with no preparation, no clear certainty that he really wanted to stop flying his own kite on the hill. And it wasn't, he told me—nibbling on my ear reassuringly—it wasn't that he didn't love us all, but now he owned things, now he owed things to people, to us, and it wasn't the adventure, it wasn't the way he had expected things to be. Perhaps, he thought, he should have applied for a fellowship abroad instead of marrying so young. He patted my thighs. I knew his regrets were not really personal. I was not yet hideous or hateful, the children were ours and he was as committed to tending their growth as I. They were his line, his manhood. They would have graves in the cemetery in Lenox, near his father, near his father's plot and his own. But still in the specific present moment, they did hamper our movements. To go out at all we always had to have a sitter we couldn't always afford. I was not the seventh wonder anymore. My insides had been thoroughly explored. Perhaps there was nothing left but the intertwining of limbs like old trees, reaching weakened branches out toward the sun. He was going to be a good professor, a committed, intelligent man. I love his care for history, his tidying up facts, his placing events in order and the sweeping theories he plays with, dismisses, recalls, and makes work for him. But I can see how the particular choice of me for wife, the particular children we have already birthed, disturbs him, how suddenly as in the final act of a Chekhov play, he sees himself trapped, other possibilities now closed to him. His own dreams of hunting tigers in Africa, of spending years on an archeological dig in Persia, are hanging about him like unanswered questions—

a weight he has to carry each day. Perhaps he should leave me and go to Hawaii, and live with an Oriental, who will be forever inscrutable, and hold his attention with empty eyes and swinging hips, beneath the palm trees and swaying coconuts. Perhaps we should not continue this piling up of material goods, stop sharing closets and meals, and break out in dizzy private directions. Altogether his confidences last night made me sad—I am so ordinary a person, and since the children have arrived I am even more ordinary. Where once I read poems of Baudelaire and drew large if inaccurate comparisons to Dylan Thomas, now all I do is read Benjamin Spock and quake at the knees that I am not measuring up. I too want to go to Moscow and will probably never get there.

Perhaps I should complete my master's degree and continue for the doctorate. My thesis on Jane Austen is still half done and, like unreturned library books, on my conscience. If I went on to become a professor in my own name, then if Paul leaves me for a sexy student or confesses a sudden middle-aged lust for little boys (such things have happened to other women—I cannot count on being spared) then if Jane Austen has won me a position, I can at least support myself. But Paul is today my custodian, and as of now he needs to see my reaction to his latest idea. He will not leave me while he is trying to convince me of his theories of history. Fathers are trying to kill their sons as Cronus tried to munch on Zeus, and that's why we have war each generation; as the fathers take political power, they avenge themselves on their male offspring by so constructing national fears and aspirations that war and death are inevitable. Man is so much a beast that each father hates his child for living longer, for being stronger as he starts to weaken, and the battlefield, the foxhole, the combat of youth is the paternal unconscious revenge, a way of surviving longer than his progeny. History, mythology, with a bow toward Freud—I always applaud whatever Paul says. I love to listen to his voice as he explains and picks over his ideas; the melody of thought, his thought, is like riding the waves in the ocean, the sun on your back, the pull of the undertow about your legs, and the easy rise and fall of your body pushed and pulled without any willful action on your part. I don't always concentrate on everything he says as carefully as I might, but I enjoy being spoken to. Paul, my darling, I know that things are not at a high pitch of romance. You do not feel you would die without me—in fact, certain exciting possibilities occur to you in the event of my suddenly having a heart attack while carrying home the groceries, or my being murdered by some drug addict, who only wanted to steal your typewriter which I foolishly defended with my life. A car escorting the prime minister on a tour of Harlem might run me over as I was crossing Broadway, having gone to the drugstore to pick up a pack of cigarettes for you. Still, when I see you sleeping and I run my fingers across your back and I touch your hair and I finally kiss you and prod you, and you open your eyes and you see me, like the New England landscape of your childhood, familiarity masking profound mystery, unextraordinary but yours, and you reach up to me—each time I feel a fullness, a completeness. We, perspiring in the heat, the sheets damp from our common graspings, we do, after all, have a great connection to each other.

When I was still in high school, spending hours before the mirror expecting a miracle to change what I saw there, I did not believe it possible that a man would choose to love and protect me, to create children with me. I thought I was too

peculiar, had too many evil thoughts, and was in some unde-
fined way condemned to loneliness. I said with adolescent
bravado that I didn't intend to marry, that I would become a
foreign correspondent, a witness to the political criminality of
the world. Without a formal religious commitment, from my
white bland house, my chintz wallpapered room, my high
school banner thumbtacked onto a very common bulletin
board—from all that, I developed a moral fanaticism, a
socialist politic, and I dreamed of being Lenin's mistress,
Trotsky's savior. Instead, I was delighted when Barnard College for Women accepted me, and overcome when Paul, on the
dormitory phone so everyone knew a boy had called me,
asked me out a second and then a third time.

I did not imagine on those early dates that laundry needed
sorting. I was more aware of the uniqueness of my soul than
its *commonness*. I was infatuated with the poetic images that
colored my brain, not realizing the important functions of
hands and arms, breasts and genitals—not understanding at
all that replacing the church on the mountain top, the lake, the
gray stones in the long fields, the daisies and the dandelions,
and the water bugs and June mosquitoes, I was to become the
home of Paul. I would be not so very different after all from
my mother, whose golf-playing, card-playing intellect used to
irritate me. My planned intention was to be as unlike her as
possible, but I find that I am feeding and caring, just like her,
with only a little less attention to order and propriety. I suppose that only if I had metamorphosed into a kangaroo or a
pheasant or a grasshopper would my life have been substan-
tially different from hers. There was something in the biological tie between us that destined us to be alike.

My mother I first remember by the dressing table, applying

great slabs of red lipstick to her already perfect mouth. Going out, going out too much, the adults are always leaving for dances at the country clubs, card games in the afternoon, shopping expeditions to the city in the morning, and always I am waiting and watching the road, listening to the cars on the distant concrete, waiting for the sound of wheels on the pebbles, the quick slam of brakes, the return of the person I needed, the person whose existence creates the air for survival. She would pick me up and show me all the things that she had bought, wallpaper samples, fabric swatches, shoes, dresses, play outfits—everything was always being redone. All decorations, personal and interior, were continually being made obsolete and in need of replacement. She would sit with me while I had milk and cookies and I would feel while I had her in my sight such a pleasure. In the mornings before she had breakfast, I would wait before her door, I would squat down on the floor and hold my doll and peer under the crack, hoping to see movement, proof that she was really there. How hard it was to wait, glued like a fly in a trap. How I desired to be in bed beside her, and how I despised the growing and going away from her that was forced on me by increasing age. She was my first love, my object, my darling, and when I left, all eagerness to go across the river to college, I felt like a paper doll, torn in many places, fluttering in a sharp wind. Dreadful to confess, unfashionable point among my friends, too terrible to admit to anyone, I loved my mother and still would comfort myself on any number of occasions by nestling close to her, big and aged as I am, but of course I can't even covertly show her I am still available.

OUT OF WEEK THREE

The idea first occurred to me when I was resting on the bed in the hospital reserved for interns on the night shift. The day had been long and the night endless and I was suffering from the universal complaint of interns, fatigue, painful fatigue. Perhaps that in itself explained the freedom and creative movement of my mind, as if alertness in itself required pre-conceptions and dull ordered ways of looking at things. I started to think about the mongoloid born that morning on the OB ward. Doctor G. had identified the defect within ten minutes of birth, the mother still knocked out from the ancsthetic, the father proudly making telephone calls on the floor below. Nothing to do. Bad protoplasm, he said, scowling at the mother as if she were responsible for the disaster mewing softly in his hands. I intend to be a pediatrician, and have worked now for ten years toward that end, ten years because I took time out for Paul and the children, but Paul has understood. I always have to return, however little of myself I could give to him and Elizabeth and the baby. I have a housekeeper who cooks and cleans and covers for me at the

87

odd hours of the day and night I have to be in classes or at the hospital. They want more of me at home, arranging flowers, cooking in big pots, but I have forced myself to be ruthless and leave at my appointed time. I am a woman determined to be of value, of social use, a skilled and particular tool. I intend at the end of my residency to practice in some area where I am needed. I will give oral polio vaccines, make TB tests, treat worms and rickets and measles, mumps, leukemia, tumors, and attempt to give as good care to the poor as they could buy with the winnings of a sweepstakes ticket.

Paul knew that about me when we married and he has only on rare occasions complained: when I missed his sister's wedding in Boston—when the housekeeper quit and he had to take over for a month before a suitable replacement could be found. He knew that although I loved him I was not the kind of woman who could or would serve my entire life, like a platter of food, over to any eager eater. I was not a wilting princess whose father rides out, combing the neighborhood for royal suitors. I had brave intentions: feminist or not, disapproved of by ladies' magazines and mental health experts or not, I planned to be bold and dare to consider myself extremely important—and that's what's pushed me all these years through college, through medical school, completing courses, papers, laboratory work in the wee hours of the morning, in order to be a person with a name and a title and an income potential (should I wish it) of my own.

But the idea I had concerned the mongoloid, not the first I'd seen, but cutting at me through all the defenses I've necessarily built—the walls between me and the parents—its eyes so slanted, its nose so flat, its brain cells slanted, leaning against each other weakened—and then I thought of the miscarriage, the dead fetus already packed in a small box in the morgue in the basement. Around noon a seventeen-year-old had lost a six-month baby—she seemed relieved. Welfare would be delighted, and the dead child had avoided what was at best a difficult situation. Still, the baby's little face was perfect and its brain no doubt fine. What if—here's the idea—we took the brain cells of the fetus, the embryo, dead a few mere hours, and transplanted them in the head of the mongoloid—would not a new, a healthy brain grow? Now of course every first-year student knows nerve tissue does not regenerate and therefore cannot be transplanted from one organism to another, but that applies to adult nerve tissue. The fetus must be more supple, adaptable, not yet used to one chemical house; perhaps it could be induced to change locales and reproduce itself in other circumstances. We could take the entire brain and insert it within the shell of the Mongoloid and then reproduce womb conditions for a period of time. With chemical aid perhaps the transplanted brain would take root and prosper—an end to defective children. I mulled over the proposition for a while, spoke to a friend in the research laboratory, and we started to experiment the following week. Very quickly we discovered that it wouldn't work.

I was discouraged, of course. Naturally I knew what the odds against me were, but still with a kind of dogged hope I persisted in a silent expectation that the baby rats would survive. As they quickly—some instantly—stopped vital functions, I faced what could only be called total defeat. Perhaps this episode of overblown ambition in the laboratory explains my mood and odd participation in what follows. The end result of all these events has been to cause me to question my fundamental abilities as a doctor.

I had emergency room duty the night of June 18th. Despite a full day's work, I had rushed home to say good night to Paul and the baby and Elizabeth. As I closed the door, I could see Paul reading to his daughter a Babar book he had just bought her. I wished for a brief moment to stay home with them. When I got to the hospital, the early evening daylight seemed ominous in the near-empty facilities. The light was too bright for the eight o'clock hour, and the white tiled floors and walls illumined by the bare electric bulbs that were turned on by automatic switch in the basement seemed like a surrealistic setting. And so in a way it was. The first few patients were routine. A kid with a bloody nose his hysterical mother couldn't control; an old man with stomach pains needing further observation; a diabetic woman with leg swelling— easy work, a view of humanity as the recipient of nothing but pain and disaster—a closed-in world in which I am an assistant god. I am healthy and clean and white, and I have learned to have a voice that is concerned with but not overwhelmed or horrified by whatever is brought before me.

But then around ten o'clock there appeared on my turn as admitting doctor a young Puerto Rican girl, some seven or eight years old. Her mother, an attractive young woman, crossing herself and crossing herself silently, looked at her daughter with wild eyes. And with them came a priest. I knew this priest slightly because he had come to a staff meeting to discuss the narcotics program in the neighborhood and the children's health-care plans, and to beg us to stay in the area and not become millionaire doctors with fat suburban practices. He was a good-guy priest, a people's man of the cloth. He was very calm as he explained the immediate medical problem to me. Nonia had come to her mother earlier in the evening with a story of the Virgin Mary's having appeared before her in the elevator as she was on her way up to their apartment. The Holy Virgin, according to the child, held out her arms and kissed her on both hands, telling her that she was the most blessed in all the 110th Street parish and that she would be rewarded with a special gift.

The mother had at first laughed at the child's story. "Who ever," she said, "had heard of a saint in a New York housing project—it's probably against the law or something"—but then the child held out to her mother her small hands, turning them upward so she could see on the palms two small wounds from which blood oozed at a steady if not violent pace. The mother had snatched the child up and run to the priest, who explained to me that he had attempted to stop the bleeding with handkerchiefs and tissues but had not succeeded.

"Of course," he said to me, "this is clearly a case of hysteria. This little girl attends the parochial school and some sensitive children react badly to the perhaps overly vivid descriptions of some of our more fanciful older nuns. You know how it is," he said to me with an apologetic shrug of his liberal shoulders.

"What about the mother, what does she think? What do you think?" I asked her. She replied: "My daughter is a good girl. Take away, Doctor, please take away her stigmata so she can go back to school—only one more week and she graduates to the third grade—she is nothing wrong in the head—*fix!*— bandages, something!" she demanded of me.

Of course it's hysteria, I thought. Must have follow-up psychologicals done on the child; a social worker had best investigate the home situation. I turned to the girl after writing a few basic facts on the chart. She was wearing Mary Janes with pink socks now blood-speckled. She had on a pretty polka-dotted dress with a little crinoline underneath. Her small face looked up at mine shyly, and then she said, "Mama doesn't believe me, nor the Father, but maybe you will. The Virgin came to me and she smiled." Nonia smiled herself in ecstasy, pleasure, a curiously unchildlike joy. She was a vision-seer, one of those whose gifts are perhaps extra-ordinary. There was a nice gentle pride in the way she held her hands out to me, palms upward. I saw the tiny wounds, not jagged as if cut by an irregular object, but small openings in the tissue, like gills on a fish, and a small red stain of fresh blood gathering about the wrist. I looked at the innocent eyes and I heard the priest say, "Tranquilizers, Doctor. I do think that if you attack the basic hysteria the symptoms will subside. I can give you family background on the child later, and I'm sure that will be requested in any follow-up care you intend to give." First I felt an intern's annoyance at his playing doctor, diagnosing and prescribing ahead of me. Obviously I was the authority on the scene and then the strangest thing happened—I remembered my sophomore-year trip abroad.

. . .

Five Barnard girls with over $1500 between us, and we were very serious. We went to every church and every museum and we bought picture postcards of our favorites. We hitchhiked and youth-hosteled and drank beer with boys of all nations in cafés. We felt free and adult and like young conquerors on the soil of an aging, dying civilization—and at the same time we felt awed and dwarfed by the many miracles man had made, by the languages and the cathedrals and the Gothic arches and the Renaissance doorknobs, and if it had not been that we were all friends and kept each other's spirits up, there would have been many times when the size and variety of the continent would have made each of us despondent in our single unimportance.

Still I retained from that trip and from several art history lectures I attended in the following years an image of the Virgin Mary in her blue robe with her arms open, her eyes clear and her skin pale and marbled. I could see her receiving the homunculus as the rays of God entered her right ear, as she knelt at her morning prayers, and later the Archangel telling her the news as she sits impassively on an embroidered stool—the Nativity, the Adoration, the deep blues of the illuminated medieval manuscripts, the sad eyes of the Renaissance madonnas, the rigid, tight-lipped Virgins of the north; the Crucifixion, the Pietà, the Assumption, when at last she rises, still impassive on clouds of silver, surrounded by cherubim and seraphim, her hands raised in ritual blessing, Mother of Christ taken at last to her Son. I saw it so clearly that suddenly it seemed impossible to be certain she had not appeared in the housing project on 110th Street to this little girl who could after all be a saint.

Rationality, years of healthy skepticism crumbled before a more primitive knowledge; things lurked in the closet of my childhood, ghosts, goblins, blue fairies and pink ones flittered about the lawn, and monsters with blood dripping from five-foot fangs lumbered across the Jersey marshlands not far from my suburban comfort. And if I had stopped believing in things I could not confirm with sight or touch or reason, a portion remained, a mystical whining of the spirit unsatisfied with classes in anatomy and biology; and then the further questions, certain ironies always present.

So much I had accepted on faith that belongs supposedly to the technological, rational society—for example, protons and electrons, molecules bumping about, controlled by electrical pulls to positive or negative poles—splitting, fusing, so small that no one can see them, just deduce their existence from their works. Well, the same was said of God and His angels centuries before, and I had laughed in sophomoric superiority at Aquinas, Augustus, St. Bernard and all his steps of humility, and still I sat and took down as fact in notebooks filled with intense scrawls the names of unpronounceable substances whose blackboard existence was unconvincing— such substances as $(NH_4)_2$ (SO_4) Cu_3 $(PO_4)_2$, FE $(HCO_3)_3$. All these numbers represent substances, something real. Do they or don't they? I have never seen them. I have heard one professor or another describe them. I have also heard described unseeable waves that run through the air transporting sound or pictures on electricity's wanton back. I constantly accept as fact things I cannot personally confirm or deny. I have been told that electricity will stay in the wires, that it will not run amok among the walls, but I don't know this for a fact. Science has gone beyond the scope of individual knowledge and hangs now in the religious way like a cloud above our heads that we take to be the complete and entire sky. As I stood there wondering, the priest began to insist I summon the staff psychologist; the mother weeping with shame, the little girl staring straight ahead with big black luminous eyes fixed on some far point beyond the confines of the examining room—suddenly I didn't know if I believed in molecules or incubi, one or the other or neither. Just at the moment when I would have had to make a professional pronouncement or stall for time by calling in the resident who was sleeping in a room at the end of the corridor, a young man burst into the room, calling for his mother in Spanish, English and street talk.

He had found us through the receptionist; he knew we were here through the neighbors who had gathered in the laundry room in the basement to discuss Nonia's condition. But he was shaking. "My orange juice, Momma, who took my orange juice—I must have it now." And soon with the priest and me questioning him, it became clear. He had returned from the clinic and left his evening's dose of Methadone and orange juice in the icebox; he had returned after a pleasant day in the park with friends to find his Methadone gone and the paper cup crumpled in the garbage can. The stigmata were indeed the work of a drugged mind pulling open suggestible skin. I knew then of course how to proceed, and ordered the proper medicines to counteract the drug the child had taken; I ordered tests and had the child removed to the children's ward to be aided in as fast a return to sanity as possible. But then as the priest was launching into a long discussion on the problems of addiction in the neighborhood and the necessity for medical and theological personnel to unite on an attack on the social virus, I felt disappointed that a true voice from beyond human reach had not spoken to us and reaffirmed the mysteries. I doctored all the rest of the night the best I could, always frightened my inexperience would harm someone, and yet simultaneously confident my inherent good qualities would make error impossible.

In the early hours of the morning I left the hospital, out

through the subbasement and past the coffee shop where two policemen were dunking donuts and writing reports, past the orderlies sloshing the floor with muddy water and pushing stringy mops along the green tiles, past the X-ray rooms, the auditorium with its red velvet curtains, donated by the wife of the chief surgeon, past the directional signs and metal carts piled up beside the quiet kitchen, and into the hot air of the street. I was wearing my white coat and carrying my purse close to my body, hoping to discourage any lurking snatchers, any muggers who had not yet folded up for the night. I listened to my footsteps on the street, afraid to hear an echo, to find myself followed. I wished I could hit, punch or karate any would-be attacker, but I knew certainly that whatever the equality of my education, status, economic power might be, my body was vulnerable, and could be crumpled, bruised, entered by whatever violator should chance to find me walking down his street. I hurried home to Paul, climbed into bed, exhausted with the night's work. I fell asleep and dreamt that I was sinking in quicksand and that God sent an angel who reached out a strong arm to pull me to safety, but when I grasped the arm it turned into a telescope, and as I sank, I looked through the lens and saw the stars, like germs on the slides in biology class, wriggling, a stratosphere or two away.

IN WEEK FOUR

Soap, Ivory 3 bars
Ajax
Mr. Clean
Animal crackers
2 jars strained beef
2 jars strained lamb
2 jars strained peas
2 jars strained egg yolk
Cigarillos
Brillo pads
Toothpaste
Shampoo
Frozen lasagne
Frozen peas
Frozen pork with bean sprouts
2 gallons milk
2 Tropicana orange juice
1 Mr. Bubble-bath

I love pop art. I regret its fading from the scene. How perfect it was to be recognized and appreciated by the artists. Like a nun in medieval France, there was a while when I felt my interior world represented in the museums and all the proper public places. Rigid people laughed, not seeing that pop art is the perfect legitimatization of life itself, a landscape art of the contemporary scene, a glorification of the inner mind, a portrait of the soul. What else should art be about? A Winnie-the-Pooh head stares at me from the cereal box. What gargoyle on top of a Romanesque church could have told more about the spirit of the artist and the age? They ought to give right of sanctuary in supermarkets and let all of us be safe from police, FBI, tax agents, if we are in the marketplace purchasing something.

Paul says that we will not sell out, not give up our souls for cars and color television, and a home with a lawn near a county shopping center. He says that we must be like his New England ancestors, devotional and determined in the pursuit of truth and simple in our tastes, and I am agreed, though I find myself wavering sometimes in purpose, and once I dreamed I had a charge account at Saks Fifth Avenue and went on a hilarious buying spree. I charged and sent home ten pairs of shoes, dozens of $150 dresses, long negligees, costume jewelry, silk scarves, perfumes, chain belts—enough to make a happy courtesan out of any puritan. In the dream I bought an ounce of facial cream for $80, and I had my hair set in ringlets, and I had on an original hat by Mr. John. I was a terrible trollop in that dream. And I suppose I must confess to other lusts. My mother sometimes takes me to lunch at fancy restaurants and I pretend I am a member of the jet set or international society as I order in my school French. I am always a little ashamed of my middle-classness—to be poor and desperate or rich and corrupt would seem a more distinguished position on the social ladder, but I must content myself with Jell-O chocolate pudding for dessert, not mousse, and remember my station. In America, of course, any mobility is theoretically possible, so I have only myself to blame if I have not passed from Paramus High School to the Princess Borghese's inner circle. I could have been anyone, a Playboy bunny, an industrialist's diamond-studded wife, a librarian in the Oshkosh Public Library. . . . The fact that I am what I am is by my own choosing, and remains so for the rest of my life, since radical options continue to be open. What a dreadful responsibility. Choice is so difficult and bound to leave you burdened with a million regrets. I am after all nothing but a soft plastic peg and could be made to fit into any size or shape hole.

My mother did send the maid last week, and with a disapproving set to her lips, she cleaned and scrubbed every corner of the apartment. She wiped days of accumulation of cereal crust off the baby's highchair, vacuumed dust from the closet floor, found stray underpants and a pair of winter boots I thought I had lost forever; she defrosted the icebox and waxed the floor and found a place for all the trappings of our life — the pens, the papers, the journals were put on a shelf. Rhinestone earrings I had stashed away in the cookie jar were returned to my bureau drawer. It was beautiful, the apartment was beautiful. Paul was so happy he nearly cried with relief. He couldn't wait to get me in bed—his appetite improved by the clean sheets in our purified bedroom.

As I was fighting with Elizabeth, who refused to brush her teeth with the new green brush I had just bought, I saw a serious problem. The maid was bliss, heaven, joy itself. She was competence and perfection where I was all bumblethumbs, a daydreamer, an alien stranger; but to employ a servant, Paul and I both felt, was a tacit acceptance of the inequalities in our political social system. Why should she scrub while I had leisure? Why should she need to work for minimal wages whereas I did not? The inequity could not sit well on my conscience. Maybe the time will come when machines, robot maids, could do the necessary work, but in the meantime, could I become a capitalist exploiter, could I take unfair advantage of my race and education to hire another to do the necessary chores? Of course not—I would never succumb. At least I hoped I wouldn't bend in my determination, but it grieved me terribly to tell my mother I didn't want the maid to come back the following week.

Last night we hired a babysitter, one of the fatter Barnard students who wouldn't have a date on a Saturday night, and we went off to the Stanleys' party. As we walked along Riverside Drive, we stopped at the monument for soldiers and sailors—climbing its steps, we looked out over the Hudson to the shores of New Jersey. The Palisades Amusement Park lights glittered like those of an oil field. Paul put his arm around me and we kissed in front of the children in the street and the black men playing cards on the steps of the nearby brownstone and the old lady walking an aged mongrel dog. We behaved as if we were in Paris, where people kiss and urinate on the corners of each street. It seemed as we walked along the shabby Drive that we had the city in the palm of our hand, that we could do anything, be anything, fly on our own power. It was a curious euphoria, as if we were lovers in a musical comedy in which there was no dimension of age and our smiles would freeze on our faces behind the last curtain in a kind of theatrical immortality. We reached the Stanleys' house and went up in the green-painted self-service elevator that creaked and groaned as it passed each floor. The heavy gate opened onto a long hallway in which there was a faint smell of garbage. (Lots of the buildings along the Upper Drive share that peculiar smell. It's a place the rich deserted a generation ago, leaving the high ceilings and the view of the George Washington Bridge to us.)

At the Stanleys' we found the party already in motion. A young editor and his sari-wrapped Indian bride talked to me about American women, how coarse, ambitious and unfeminine they are—how they are overeducated and overdressed. It was hard to disagree: mea culpa, mea culpa. I moved to another part of the room. I discussed Marxism with an intense graduate student whose field turned out to be medieval literature. I chatted with an old friend about the children, and we planned to ask the Park Commissioner to build more sprinklers in the playground. There is no need now to be so sparing of water. I drank just enough of my drink (I could taste the wax of the paper cup with the Scotch) to coat my natural shyness.

Judy Stanley told me they're planning to move to New Jersey since Ed got that appointment at Rutgers. I saw the house they would live in, the lawn and the garden furniture, the supermarket in the shopping center with shelf after shelf of colored toilet tissues—pinks, blues, mauves and yellows, so that all conceivable walls could be neatly matched. I started to talk about the pollution in the rivers all the paper dyes are causing. I had read in an article in *Scientific American* that the dyes were turning our rivers into poisonous beds of seething chemicals. It wasn't at all necessary; we could all use white toilet paper, white stationery, white paper towels, and the water would be purer. And then I heard myself sounding too concerned, so I stopped and returned to a less contentious subject. We talked about the war, but what really was there to say? We all agreed, we were all impotent. A man who was writing a book on the Mideast told me that the newest weapons were a kind of bomb that released over a large area a gas that damaged brain cells but left motor activity untouched. The government was pleased because it had found a non-lethal way of killing.

I had once seen a film sequence about a woman who was having her face lifted in one of those swanky sanitariums. They had stripped the covering skin off all her features, leaving exposed raw flesh, pink and bleeding. The woman lay in bed, her hands tied down, so she would not accidentally touch and contaminate her face. She stared helplessly into the camera that explored slowly the pitiful results of her excessive vanity. I feel somehow like that when we talk of the war. I looked over to the bar, and there standing with one foot on the seat of Jamey Stanley's tricycle was my husband. He was talking to a small girl with big eyes and all sorts of other exaggerated equipment. I could hear him talking about his book. I knew he was explaining to her his thesis, proved beyond any question by a careful examination of history, that revolutions have always been betrayed, that idealism has turned inevitably into dictatorship, and that humanitarianism, when believed in passionately, has resulted in cruelties beyond the imagining of dispassionate moderates. A bureaucracy, a power struggle, has followed each revolutionary victory, and the very people whose rights were initially violated are once again raped, but this time by their own leaders. The human being is too corrupt, too greedy, too hungry, for revolution to succeed. The little girl was dazzled—probably a graduate student specializing in Oriental pottery. She was all excited at being given so much historical truth in one evening, and he, still with the euphoria we had shared earlier in the evening, was delighted with a new audience, a new convert to his historical realism, and a new female to admire his male feathers, fluttering and fluffing as they were in the far corner of the room.

Suddenly I felt like a drab brown sparrow. I could almost smell the orange juice that had been spit up on my shoulder that morning. I could feel that my hair needed washing and my hands some hormone cream to eradicate the effects of too many detergents. I talked on with as much animation as I could muster, but all the time my concentration was on him in the corner. I felt like a ship whose captain has deserted, the waves of the sea sucking me down. I would be engulfed, left to rot on the ocean's bottom, host to slithery, slimy creatures who would make my ruin their home. I wanted to go over to him, to make that intimate conversation a threesome, but I knew better than to interrupt. I contained myself by evaluating rather nastily certain former Barnard professors with an ex-classmate who was now a secretary in a television producer's office. I remembered her when she wore sneakers and blue jeans and long silver earrings. Now she looked like a total stranger with her matching alligator bag and shoes. I suppose she has matured—no revolution lasts, even private ones, is what he would have said.

At last (after I had danced in the hall where the Stanleys' stereo was blaring and the lights were out, as they used to be at parties when I was a high school sophomore, necking and petting behind the sofa of some unsuspecting Paramus matron) I walked over to where Paul and the girl were still standing, now sharing some private joke between them. I suggested it was time to go. He was reluctant, but it was past the hour we had promised the babysitter she would be released, and he dragged himself away from what he described in the elevator as a glorious party, the best we had been to in years. He spoke of what a fine friend and scholar Ed Stanley was. I was silent all the way up Riverside Drive and I wouldn't let him hold my hand. The night air felt somewhat cooler, or perhaps it was just good to be rid of the smoke and the smell of perspiring bodies. Once out on the street, things didn't seem as desperate as they had upstairs. Still, now that I was going home with him safely beside me, I felt angry that he should have made me suffer. "In not needing a particular male body, a *woman* saves herself from so many minor wounds," I said. "You mean you were jealous." He laughed. "I'm glad you get jealous." And so we went to bed. I forgave him my temporary discomfort, and he forgave me the fierce thoughts with which I had punished him, for what, after all, was a party compared to the pleasures that came after it? However, before I fell asleep, I had one final thought about his book. I won't tell him, as he would find me absurd, but I'm certain that, despite his historical evidence, revolutions must take place and one day one of them will be led by a real hero who will neither sell out his cause nor find himself knifed in the back. Some day there will be a revolution with genuine heroes and the way of life for that country will change and the air will be clean. If I don't believe in that possibility, then I see only total desolation ahead, as one power after another fights and destroys, ultimately killing us all. His book with all its historical realities will not convince me otherwise. To hold such a romantic view is obviously foolish—to believe in the good hero, virtue triumphant, is the stuff of bad television dramas and children's cartoons. But if I ignore that possibility, the alternatives are terrifying. A realistic politic would bend before the harshness of human nature, primitive man chasing primitive man with a club. Somebody has to believe in angels—the flower children are in this sense right, too much sophistication is its own gas chamber.

This morning in the supermarket we nearly had some serious trouble. I was standing in line, my cart piled high, Elizabeth perched on the seat. The baby had been left with a neighbor. Behind me came a seedy black man with an orange shirt and black porkpie hat all covered with dust. He was pushing a cart containing two six-packs of beer. "I wanna get outa here," he snarled. "I'm getting ahead of you, outa my way." I didn't have any intention of arguing and started to push my cart to one side. I suppose I was anxious and as I pushed forward I caught the metal base of the cart in front of me. At first I didn't realize what was wrong and just pulled and thrust my whole weight against the metal handle in the hopes of moving away from the angry voice behind me. "You let me through," he started to scream. "I gotta get outa here." The woman ahead of me tried to pull her cart free of mine. She, too, fluttered and jerked without actually releasing the carts. Elizabeth started to cry. I didn't want to stop to comfort her until I had gotten away. "Goddam white bitch, think you own the world, think you can just make everyone stand behind you. Yes ma'am, yes ma'am, get outta ma way." He lurched from side to side. Everyone was watching—for a few more seconds the woman and I tugged at our carts, the man yelled, Elizabeth cried. At last the manager came over and with him a policeman. Thank God, a black policeman; a little less to feel guilty about. The cop took the man out of the store, the manager disentangled our wheels, and in another ten minutes we were out on the street, the stroller piled high with groceries, Elizabeth sucking a large red lollipop, tear stains on her face, and I quite shaken. It is clear that whatever my personal inclinations, whatever our interests in the Black Panthers, our commitment to VISTA, to poverty planning, the Young Lords, the old Patriots, Harlem Prep et cetera, when the revolution comes, my head will roll. They'll probably set up a guillotine at 116th and Broadway with parade benches lining the sides of the street. Just before I am decapitated, spilling my blood across Broadway, I'll call out my innocence and the crowd will roar with laughter and call for the next white culprit to be brought before the only tribunal whose word they honor. In New Jersey, in Paramus, we never knew what was happening across the river in the city. I had never seen a prostitute, an addict, a woman on welfare, or a dishwasher blowing his top on Saturday night. Sometimes I want to go back, maybe just for a month or so, to Paramus and feel it proper to enjoy what pleasures are available, to eat without any face staring in at the window. But, of course, I'm not sure anymore whose face is at the window, perhaps it's my own. I walk between Amsterdam and Columbus and I am the stranger. They whisper and laugh and huddle together, and I am the foreigner who has no right to share their intimacies, their noise. I can just see my severed head buried beneath back issues of the Sunday *Times* as soul music blasts the walls of Columbia University down, like Jericho reduced to rubble, and bongo drums surge as loud as police sirens and ambulance horns chasing up and down the avenue.

I told Paul about the man in the market, and he thought I

should not have tried to give up my place in line but should have stood firm—a matter of principle, it was my right, et cetera—it was a terrible, cowardly example to set for Elizabeth, and on and on he went. I was relieved that I had been in the line and not he. It is sometimes both easier and safer to be a woman, one's only task to concede graciously and swiftly—no need to assert territorial claim, an upright position, and all the ghastly things that cause people to get stabbed on the streets of the city from time to time. Later when he went off to the library, his briefcase barely closing, we went out to the park.

In the midst of the cement circle a fountain sprayed cool water high into the air. Some children had no bathing suits, and others ran in and out of the wet puddles, nothing covering them but their underwear. Pails were filled and dumped. Some of the children were afraid and stood timidly at the edge watching the others. But Elizabeth immediately tugged at her pinafore until it was on the ground. I helped her remove her sneakers and off she ran. I asked her to bring me a pail of cool water so I could wet my face and hands. She forgot. The baby is crawling near the water. His legs and arms are black with dirt and his diaper is streaked with multicolored stains. He has found a puddle and splashes his hands in pleasure in the greasy water. I have not brought a towel, but in this heat the children can dry themselves in the sun. I am hot and suddenly sad. I remember when I swam in our community pool, when I turned and twisted and jumped in and out of the water. I used to have a kind of mindless pleasure in moving each limb through the water, and now I just sit and watch. I attend the children who enjoy the same glorious pleasures I once had. I sit stiff and proper, not able to run in the falling spray. Even if we should go to a pool now, I'd need company, conversation, and adult play. My brain doesn't stop orienting itself, worrying, examining or thinking. I have grown older than I ever intended.

I've been thinking about Amelia Earhart. She wasn't really a woman, not as the magazines and the mental hygiene experts would have it. She was too comfortable with a greasy machine —too anxious for challenge and exploration. She needed to be somewhere first, ahead of everyone else. She may have been cranky and irritable in petty matters. She may have been content only when she was alone in the sky where the single compromise forced upon her would be death, obliteration, in which she would find equality at last in the open spaces she must have both feared and loved. I'm not at all like that. I am afraid of the emptiness of the sky, and I'm afraid when I stand on mountains and look down at craggy ravines. I'm afraid I'll fall and be crushed. I don't really feel exhilarated by the scenery. I just feel uncertain and want very much to hold Paul's hand, lean against him and return to some flat, dull place that doesn't threaten my equilibrium or overwhelm me with its significance or beauty. Perhaps that's a result of growing up in a suburban area where no rock is too jagged, no climb too steep, and there are well-kept paths through the woods. Moderation may have become part of my physiology, as necessary as water to a fish.

OUT OF WEEK FOUR

At first when I heard of the organization I thought Another Mother for Peace was a kind of sweet joke, a version of my mother's garden club which raised money through an annual fair for the local hospital. I thought of myself as a member of the avant-garde in all fields and didn't like the image of myself with a little white hat plastered on my head while I wrote cute letters with sincere rhetoric to my congressman who was as powerless to control the barbarians as Elizabeth or the baby. But then Paul and I talked it over. "Start where you can," he said. "The individual is ineffective, a speck, algae in the sea, but a gaggle of you ladies—who knows!" He laughed condescendingly, and at that moment I decided to join the group, give it my all—"Betsy Ross, Florence Nightingale, Mme. Curie, Jane Addams, Helen Keller, Carry Nation, Gertrude Stein, Eleanor Roosevelt," I muttered at him, recalling a childhood of biographies designed to return pride to the little girl and give her hope that with incredible brains, wit and determination, sacrifice and pain, she too might make a worthy contribution to improving or at least tempering the human condition.

That's what I'm doing here in Vietnam—demonstrating to all that I am to be taken seriously—what I feel and what I think, multiplied by all the others like me (since I joined the organization our membership, due to my efforts, has increased 800%), what I want, deserves to be attended to. I am as important now as any representative of a large group, as a Mafia member with a Supreme Court judge in his hip pocket, or the owner of a radio station, or a vice president of CBS, or the *Times* correspondent in Washington, or a labor leader, honest or dishonest.

I am no longer Margaret Reynolds who just sits in the playground with her children, despairing when she has time to think about it, despairing about the war, the insanity of the arms race, the creeping madness of the crawling fascists who everywhere ride around in police cars topped with our flag, decals on their side windows of our flag. Anyway, that's one of the points I made at our last meeting. I addressed 3000 ladies in the Felt Forum in Madison Square Garden, and I thanked them for sending me and Dora Grossbart to Vietnam to observe for ourselves the behavior of our soldiers and the conditions of this war, and to attempt to bring some word to the front of the vitality and growing popularity of the peace movement. "Lay down your arms—don't kill anyone"—that's what we intend to tell the boys when we meet them. Not directly, of course, but through the organization we represent, its large numbers alone enough to force some kind of attention. Dora says that we must try to believe that most of the soldiers would rather be in the States, in school or lurking on the corner, being a menace in their home town streets, than here killing and being killed.

I'm not so sure about that. Dora, who has become my best

friend since I started working almost full time for Another Mother for Peace, has a way of believing the best of people all the time. She has doggedly and optimistically worked for a series of losers from Henry Wallace to Adlai Stevenson and on to Eugene McCarthy. Even before that she cheered the Lincoln Brigade off to its gory end, and through it all she has gained an enormous amount of political know-how. She can fund-raise the feathers off a peacock, fill a rally with recording stars, and smile up at the police in a way that fends off immediate attack. But I sometimes disagree with Dora about the possibilities of humanism gaining ground.

The night is clear, and from the small window of the hotel room I can see some of the same constellations I identified as a child in New Jersey. The sounds from the street are not the tinkly Oriental ones I would have imagined. Jeeps, heavy trucks, Volkswagens and soldiers laughing and shouting. Girls fluttering on spike heels so high as to nearly cripple, and then across from the hotel, a nunnery. Every hour the bells chime. Earlier I had heard the Latin chants of the cloistered ladies as they walked from their inner courtyard into their abbey. The Reverend Mother is European, the hotel clerk told me, but the convent corps is recruited from upper-class Vietnamese families. Young girls with bodies like willow branches are draped in yards of imported black cloth and imprisoned with the Bon Dieu forever. The convent was once the mansion of a French merchant who has long since taken his tapestries and his family and returned home, bitterly decrying the pirouettes of a history that has deprived him of its bounty.

When I think of those young ladies in the cloister, I get quite cold with anger. Their lives are now committed to maintaining an illusion of spiritual fulfillment, salvation or what-not, when all around them the real earth has such acute needs and could use their hands and minds to undo the viciousness their Lord has somehow permitted. Dora says that someday when we have time we should give some thought to organizing the convents, opening them to the public demand, insisting that the buildings be used for poor children's breakfast programs and things like that.

At dinner last night we talked about our plans to travel to the front. The army had assigned us a Vietnamese guide, a press sergeant, a car and two privates to take us about. Of course this cooperation had come because our Mothers for Peace wrote both to their congressmen and the Pentagon, threatening a caravan of baby carriages blocking all traffic across the Potomac. The police, with clubs and paddy wagons, could naturally remove the mothers, babies, balloons and lollipops from the area, but the resulting worldwide publicity would have been enough to make even a Dr. Strangelove shudder.

So Dora and I received our passports, arrangements for our care were grudgingly made and we, only mildly terrified of land mines, assassins, Viet Cong and Green Berets, planned to see for ourselves how our boys felt and acted in this war. After dinner, as we had our coffee in the lobby, a beggar in the street knocked on the window near our table. He beckoned to us and naturally we looked away and speeded up the talk between us. As I was trying not to notice the increased grimaces on the beggar's face and the knocking on the window, Dora, whose moral courage is stronger than mine, said, "We are here to learn things. Let's go." So we left our table, went through the revolving doors out into the hot street, where the heavy smell of garbage and sewerage took some getting used to before I breathed naturally. The beggar said he would exchange a story for dollars and it seemed as good a thing to buy as anything else. So we listened, we two American ladies leaning against the side of the building, as he told and half sung in near-perfect English his tale.

In the province of Liu, a long time ago before the Europeans had even imagined the landscape of Asia, the Emperor Tu ruled with an iron hand, commanding extraordinary duties from all his subjects. He taxed them hard and required of all men and women two weeks of labor in each season of the year. All the subjects of the province of Liu looked forward to the time when the tyrannical Emperor would die and his daughter Lia, known to all for her gentle manner, if very simple mind, would rule in his place. Lia grew to be a beautiful woman, but she was unwilling to choose a husband from among the nobles of the court. She had remained so like a child in her mind and she spoke to hardly anyone, and seemed interested only in the cultivation of the beautiful white flowers that blossomed year-long in her garden. The Emperor Tu declared that she must make a choice. He designed a contest in which the winner would take her as his prize. All males of distinguished families were eligible to compete. A fight among male birds was planned for a day in early June.

It was the custom in those times for every young man to train one of the multicolored, bandylegged roosters to fight in his name, and in the villages there were bird-fights on all feast days and religious holidays.

Several of the young nobles aspired to guide the ruling hand and hoped to win the beautiful Lia and the gifts she could deliver to her bridegroom. They carefully picked and trained their birds, putting their own spit into their beaks, rubbing them with incense and powders and otherwise following all the known folklore of bird care. The birds' claws were sharpened, and the birds themselves made mean by constant teasing. Their red eyes were filled with irritants to accustom them to pain and discomfort. Each of the young nobles hoped that his bird, when preened before the princess, would slash to death the others, leaving his master to take the richly endowed maiden.

On the day of the contest the princess appeared in white robes, looking pale and somber; she sat stiffly by her father's side. The birds of many colors, wearing the silver tags on which were engraved the names of the noble families of the Court, began to fight with one another in the plaza of the palace, and as all the noble world looked on, the feathers, blue and green and white, tore into the air, and the sharp claws of one bird disemboweled another, sending blood and guts across the marble floor. The dead birds, swept by the keepers of the grounds, piled high by the princess' feet. After the Court had returned from a recess in which they drank and ate, the fight continued. Finally, only two birds were left; the princess stared at both clawing, shrieking birds, and perhaps in her confused mind she thought she must wed one bloody bird and take his stained claws and sharp beaded feathered body to her marital bed. She excused herself from her father's side for a moment, and while the victor-bird was dancing madly about the pierced chest of his sinking enemy, the Princess Lia took a pearl-handled knife and slit her throat among the white flowers she had so dearly loved.

After this there was a riot in the land and the peasants reduced the palace of Tu to ashes. It was on that barren site, with its broken walls and remains of fine pottery hidden in the weeds, that the army of a neighboring country camped. Order was eventually restored.

At the end of this story, the beggar laughed, accepted the few dollars Dora pulled from her purse and went off down the street. We went back into the hotel and had a drink.

At night the air conditioning makes the room cold, and I sit with my notebook on my lap with the bed covers pulled close around me. I have never needed a man to protect me. I have never been forced to change direction on someone else's command. Paul and I are equals. Like Tom Sawyer and Huck Finn adventuring around the Mississippi. But now so far from home I feel as if a hunter has the sights of his gun trained at my heart. With a barely audible click, the sound of a light switch in another room, I will be punctured. When the room is dark and the shapes of the furniture are indistinct, I get a sense something will reach out from the walls, and I will fall, smashed on the floor, will be lifted into outer space to float unredeemed, a white skeleton atomizing slowly, orbiting forever, with white eternity between my bones. Child's fears, of course—I just close my eyes and ignore the abyss at the cover's edge. I remind myself over and over again, I'm a leader of women, an organizer, a radical, not a timid child, but I worry what will become of my family if I don't return—my own death is very sad. I have been inoculated against smallpox, typhoid, black plague, but still I may catch some unnamable Oriental disease and return to Riverside Drive wrapped in a shroud cheaply made in Hong Kong. The peace movement, all its factions, would hold a mass memorial, and the occasion bring political profit to everyone but me.

There are no flies in this hotel. The air conditioning works perfectly. I had always thought of Asia as crawling with insects. I brought along citronella. Perhaps I will need it in the field. I thought the hotel room would have a huge fan in it with large blades that rotated up near the ceiling at some lazy pace. I thought the sound would be like that of an airplane propeller or an outboard motor like the ones on Lake Tahoe where I went with my parents in the summer. I can't sleep here. I've tried to sleep but I can't. Perhaps I'll be able to sleep when I get closer to the war. Now the anticipation is keeping me awake. I never could sleep the night before I was to go away to camp. I couldn't sleep on trains. I very often vomited all the way to Maine. Here's a thought. What if the Lord Jehovah sent an angel to the fortress of Dienbienphu because he was concerned that men were tired of fighting for ideals, principles, and glory? The angel's job would be to encourage the battle because the Lord didn't want man to turn into an angel before his appointed time.

. . .

I'm trying to go to sleep now. My pillow is all damp from all the tossing and turning. The moon is so thin and in a space so far away. My mother does not understand my political life. She thinks Another Mother for Peace is a subversive group, undermining our elected leaders.

Tomorrow morning I will go to the Convent. The hotel clerk looked so upset when I asked him if I might visit that I have become determined to see the cloister. Perhaps the hotel clerk is a Buddhist and that's why he doesn't want me to go to the Convent. I didn't like his alternate suggestion that I take a tour of the Botanical Gardens. Why do I stay up at night writing everything down, all this trivia? I only need some political notes for speeches and articles when we return. It's an insane habit to write down the personal things. I imagine if I were a fish, I'd get my spine up against some coral and just wait to be fossilized. I seem to be a recording machine. Why do I have to be a time capsule, why am I trying to please that unborn archeologist who will come across my notebooks and no doubt become famous because of my meticulous attention to details? Perhaps this writing is a form of prayer, like the praying of some Catholics who are constantly fingering beads

and mouthing things. Maybe I'll go turn more lights on. I'll
sleep better with more lights.

．　．　．

Dora decided not to go with me to visit the convent. She
wanted to visit the poorer sections of Saigon and possibly the
high school. Our two privates and the jeep took her off for her
tour, and I just walked across the street, determined to explore
the convent.

I found it to be a beautiful rectangular building, the archi-
tecture direct from Renaissance Italy. The Oriental nuns mop
the stone floors each day, and buckets of water are carried and
emptied, so much so that cleanliness is certainly one of the
advertised virtues of the good ladies. The cloister smells of
dampness and detergent. There are jungle plants in the garden
and red and pink flowers in a window box by the abbess's
office. For the rest the austerity is familiar. The nuns walk
about with their eyes cast down and their steps seem particularly graceless. In the church connected by a black bolted door
to the Convent, the crucifix hangs above the altar exactly as in
every small town in southern Europe. When I entered, the
candles were burning, the altar cloth shone gold, and the sun
glowed behind the stained-glass window. Only the letters on
the poor box, written in the language of Vietnam, told me I
was in a foreign country.

I was shown into the abbess's office. The heavy wooden
doors were carved with panels showing figures twisting with
the pains of the damned in Hell. They had been done by a
native woodcarver, and the landscape of Hell seemed Asian

and its inhabitants Oriental. Westerners, by implication, were all in Heaven.

The abbess was glad to see me. Visitors, even non-Catholics, were always welcome in her convent. She wanted me to see the way God had brought peace to her charges, and she herself was always glad of a chance for some worldly chatter with a lady so clearly refined and educated as myself. In fact, I had come on a very important day: later in the afternoon, all of the press were to come to witness, in the holy sense of the word, a rather special event. The abbess was a liberal, she went on to explain. She believed that the church must bend and change and absorb some of the native traditions and customs, or else it would never win over the hearts and minds of the people it most dearly wanted to save. She explained that the problem of the church was that it needed to be more dramatic, more vivid, more talked about. It must compete with the more primitive, childlike religions that tend to occupy church-won ground. A zeal, borrowing its flame from some non-rational source, burned behind her gray eyes rimmed in gold-edged glasses.

As we walked through the drafty corridors that had once been warmed by heavy carpets and prize tapestries, she told me of her childhood in the South of France. Her father had been a fisherman in a Mediterranean village and she had run barefoot about the wharves catching crabs in shallow water and bringing them in little tin pails to her mother. At the age of seven she started school and it was quickly discovered that she had an uncommon talent for music. Her parents naturally found a piano and the necessary lessons beyond their simple means. The good priest of the church arranged a scholarship in one of the finer convent schools some 250 miles away.

"After the first exile," the abbess said, "there is no other." At the convent she proved an able student, a good, if not spectacular, musician, and an obedient child. Thoughts of her home finally stopped plaguing her as the features of her parents and former playmates dissolved like cloud shapes on a windy day. The church became her refuge and there she remained. I asked her what she thought her life would have been like had God not given her musical talent. She seemed not to hear my question. When the opportunity came to go to the Orient, she never hesitated—when God is with you no place is strange, or, she added, all places are equally strange. The afternoon's event might seem surprising to one who had not learned that everything must be done to convince an indifferent population of the efficacy and beauty of the Christian church. They were having a pageant of sorts, a demonstration of the dedication of her nuns and of the necessity of giving an important role in government affairs to her minority religion. The abbess glowed with such fierce intensity that I could not imagine her with a child's frailty running beside pink and blue buildings carrying a loaf of bread in one suntanned hand.

We had lunch in what must have been at one time the ballroom of the mansion. The tables were wooden and bare. The novices served the melon and bread on heavy trays. Milk was poured from a pitcher into crystal goblets, obviously left by the former owner in his haste. The meal was silent. The nuns ate without looking to the right or left, without speaking a word, as if feeding themselves was a disgraceful act. They hurried the food down. One nun sitting alone ate nothing. She looked only at the abbess's face, a small flush on her cheeks. The abbess glanced at her fondly from time to time. After lunch there was a mass in the small church. I went out on the street and smoked a cigarette. I saw groups of people waiting on the other side. My first expectation was that there would be a parade—then I realized how unlikely in such a country in time of war a parade would be. I went back into the church and waited. Members of the press began to arrive: the UP and the AP men, the man from *Life*, the *Saturday Evening Post* correspondent with whom I had spent several delightful days in New York when he was working on an article on Another Mother for Peace last winter. No one was certain what was up. Word had been sent to the Press Club that something important was about to happen at the Church of the Little Flower on Main Street. Soldiers on leave or on lunch hour breaks hung around waiting also, buying hot dogs from a stand operated by a little old lady whose son worked at the restaurant at the airport and pilfered the merchandise for his mother's profitable street stall.

Inside the cloister the nuns were kneeling in rows on the moist earth of the central garden. Their black robes and headdresses fluttered in the warm breeze. The abbess stood before her flock and, pacing back and forth on the stone steps, she spoke: "Suicide is not our way. I want you all to understand that suicide is murder, and that the Christian God never pardons murder. He and He alone gives life and takes it. No sadness, no grief is great enough to take from God his privilege to give or withhold breath. Agony, pain, desolation, or loneliness may be his curse on our mortal moment, but it is not our place to take life. Our spirits can be destroyed but the body lives as long as He wills it." Here her voice became soft. "Sacrifice, however, is another thing. Sacrifice is pleasing to God, who compliments the suffering it causes. To agree to take one's life in sacrifice is not suicide committed in petty personal despair—but an act of glory for the celebration of God and to place Him and His followers in the fields and the streets, wherever people will tell the tale of this magnificent and sweet act. Sacrifice is a superb martyrdom following in the steps of our beloved Jesus Christ. I have picked from among all my sisters the fairest and the kindest, the most gentle and the most pure—for a sacrifice must truly wound if its meaning is to vibrate to all the corners of the earth.

"You will now follow instructions; hide your private feelings behind the discipline of the church. Let your faces deny any trace of personal fear. Prove to me that you are all brides of Christ. Sustain yourselves in Him and know that today we are closer than ever before to His side—you may all be certain we will receive His beloved appreciation. Sisters, proceed."

She gave the final command, as any sergeant might to troops whose loyalty and discipline were quite beyond question. The sisters filed from the abbey into the street. I followed and joined the watching crowd. A few smiling policemen pushed the spectators back to the curbs. They waved their sticks (clubs imported from the police department of Detroit) in a menacing way, but they smiled politely all the time. Four of the sisters now broke rank and went back into the cloister, and the nun whom I had noticed sitting alone at lunch moved to the center of the street and bent her head in solitary prayer. Then she dropped to her knees, and waved her frail body from side to side as if she would bend to the ground like a young tree in a hurricane. I started to perspire through my blouse and my throat felt dry. The four nuns reappeared through the door, pushing a wide bathtub of the sort used in luxurious European hotels at the turn of the century. The bath-tub was on a dolly and the wheels squeaked over the cobble-stoned street. It seemed a long time—a child cried in the watching crowd. At last the tub was placed right in front of the swaying nun. The bathtub was filled with water. The move-ment had created a wave that spilled over the sides and stained dark the gray stones. The abbess stepped out: "As Abraham offered Isaac, as The Son was offered for us all, I give to you, Lord, for the glory of the Catholic religion, Sister Mary Louise."

She bowed her head and Sister Mary Louise rose from her knees and walked without hesitation over to the bathtub. She removed her headdress and the crowd gasped. She was not totally bald, but short black bristles stuck up on her head in spots, and she looked like a child's doll without its wig, muti-lated. She took her robe off next, and stood in a black, shape-less, ankle-length slip. Some of the soldiers laughed, a few in the crowd whistled. There was some tittering and then an expectant hush. I saw a flash of orange and gold in the bathtub and then I saw another. Sister Mary Louise removed her black stockings and her shoes and rolled up the stockings, placing them neatly in the shoes as she had been taught at the convent. Then she looked at the abbess, who nodded her head. The other nuns were now singing "Ave Maria." When they got to the second verse, Sister Mary Louise quickly sat on the porcelain edge and lowered herself in one final splash into the tub. Then there was a scream, and another, pain beyond imagining—and the crowd was silent, cold and silent. Sister Mary Louise was silent too—her head slipped beneath the water now turned red with blood, deep rich red like the sea that Moses parted.

Seconds more, and the crowd did not move—the singing went on and on. Then the abbess went over to the tub with a quick step, and she looked down and prayed with her beads in hand, and then she retired into the convent with all her brood, less one, following.

In the crowd some ladies were sobbing. There was an angry mutter, an American "Jesus Christ, what was that about?"— and a soft patter of the sound of Vietnamese words like rain on the jungle leaves; it grew louder and more excited. I followed the man from the UP, who smiled politely at the policeman, and dashed to the side of the tub. There was nothing left but bones floating in the water. No hair, no eyes, no skin, no organs, just disconnected bones, and frolicking among them eight fat, satisfied piranha fish. Their bellies were bloated with the life of Sister Mary Louise who had given herself to Catholic martyrdom. Her soul of course was already in heaven, the rest in the waste products of the piranha fish.

. . .

I told Dora what had happened when she came back to the hotel later that afternoon. At first she thought it was a story another beggar had told, but when I convinced her the events had really happened, she became very sad. "There really is no cure, the insanity is around us and within us. It's simply too great—no matter how we organize, one or two madmen will have all the power and the other lunatics will kill themselves off."

I had never heard her talk like that before. "What is it?" I asked. "What happened to you today?"

"You know," she said, "the plane that Rita Moreno's group

is organizing to bring to Vietnam to investigate the massacres—Artists of Conscience, with Sartre, Günter Grass, Picasso, Casals, and all the other musicians, authors and painters. I heard today from one of our privates that headquarters here says that if the plane flies, they'll see to it it gets shot down or has motor trouble; the Vietcong will carry the blame, but the plane will go down with all aboard."

"Well," I said, "We'll stop them."

"Perhaps," she added, "headquarters also has plans for us." We sat quietly . . .

IN WEEK FIVE

The children are playing under the water sprinkler. The afternoon shadows have made a cool place for me to sit on this far bench. Last night Paul told me he wants me to go to graduate school this fall and complete my Master's. He says I'll grow stupid and dull if I just sit in this playground day after day. I suppose he's right—nothing really happens—nothing challenges wit or demands a fine performance.

But graduate school, oh my God! He has the patience for those many books with the fine print and for the source material on microfilm—but I don't like the smell of the long halls and listening to the words, endless words about words—formulations about art, hunting for symbols and shapes or ideas, when outside the window there are immediate events that always seem to require my attention. It's probably discipline I lack. I must cultivate a love of neatly filled notebooks with thoughts in orderly sequence—"A" follows "B" and, therefore, "etc." I must find in the past some end to the restlessness of each day. Otherwise I could turn into a stone. What a catastrophe I'll be if I don't have a profession, if I don't train myself for some small use. Paul wants a woman who is absolutely devoted to him and his purposes, who tends his home and cares for his children, but who for all of that can speak knowledgeably about the little magazines and not be left behind in conversation. It's a dreadful juggling act. I'll probably have to go to graduate school and then one day I'll be one of those shining examples of teacher and wife that girl students so admire.

I could go on to graduate school in journalism, but then what? I can't take a job and leave him and the children. I can't go to conferences on underdeveloped nations. I can't follow campaign trains across the country. I can't go south for the baseball tryouts. I can barely meet a friend for lunch and go downtown and have my hair cut now and then. But, there are compensations, if he continues to hold me in his arms each night, and if he goes on touching me under the sheets, I'll make our bed a permanent transport—and I'll go a few times a week to graduate school and make little footnotes to the efforts of others, and I will not be what he called me the other night—merely a maternal pillow, growing fatter, losing feathers over the years. He does have a nasty way of putting things.

Last night while we were having dinner at Tien Tsin on 125th Street, he told me and the Carvers who joined us (John Carver just finished his thesis on the Boer War, and she's a modern dancer) that in place of revolution man will have to set up some form of computerized plan for continual improvement. A computer could understand social stress, backlash, economic balance between the elements in society and could dictate programs that all would have to concede were scientific and impartial. *I pledge allegiance to a gray-green computer and to the rationality for which it stands.* I suppose it's not impossible, but I thought as I stirred my thousand-ingredient soup that the machine must be programmed by human beings with a peculiar bias and prejudice, and that this could very well alter the decisions of the computer and so invalidate all of its rational schemes. I didn't mention this at dinner because, after all, John Carver had spent a year in Japan and he's always talking about how obedient, docile and desirable the Japanese women are, and I just didn't want to say anything to again trigger off that invidious comparison.

The Tien Tsin is at 125th Street where the subway rises out of the ground and steel supports curve across Broadway over the cobblestoned road, like a parody of the triumphal arches the Romans built to the entrance of conquered lands. Harlem, lying behind, is devastated but still rebellious, never graciously (despite severe conditions of disease and dirt) consenting to foreign rule. It is now a place where I can never go—enemy, alien, I must stay on my side of the barbed wire. After dinner we walked in the smelling summer air, turning our backs on the territory we wouldn't dare enter. We strolled past the housing developments, huge brown-brick crates piled one on top of another, like the trucks that carry chickens to their certain death. The smell from those trucks is always particularly bad.

If we grow old together, turning more and more into one thing instead of two, an exhausted many-headed Hydra that finally refuses to divide itself further—if the pattern of our lives becomes such that we are in a symbiosis, feeding only off each other—even then one of us will die before the other, and either he will wander without me like a blind man whose dog has turned mad, or I will float in our bed like a dead fish, belly up, on the surface. One of us will have to endure without the other, and what will that be?

Perhaps I should never allow anyone too close and never need anyone too much; then death is only a disappointment, not a grief. Paul at least will have his history to tell, his footnotes to sort, and, if I'm nothing but chemical particles, and the children, wrapped in the satisfactions of their own lives, pay no attention to the old man, he will turn to the library and his students and anchor himself somehow—but what will I do, when I have no special chores, no one demanding my approval, requiring my attention? I will fall like a disinherited meteor and crash on some unimportant bit of ground. Perhaps I will come to the playground and look at other people's children, watching each mother, recognizing her mistakes, perceiving all with my experienced eye, and yearning all the time for something to do. I will be like the old lady who comes to the park and sits near the old man. I will be just like her. She's not here today, perhaps it's too early or too hot, or she's gone to her rich sister in Connecticut. The old man is not here either—is it possible he's gotten sick, been taken in the middle of the night to the hospital—paralyzed by a sudden stroke? Did a neighbor hear his cry, or was he found slumped in the elevator by an irritated night clerk? Maybe he'll come later in the afternoon when the sun is less strong. Perhaps he has found an old friend and they are having coffee in Bickford's at 96th Street and Broadway. I wonder why they're not here yet.

Elizabeth comes for her doll. She wants to take it under the sprinkler with her. The baby sucks on a pretzel back in the stroller—I adjust the seat so he can lie down, and soon, as I push the wheels rhythmically back and forth, he'll sleep, paying no attention to the shouting and the running beside him. Perhaps it happened with the old man and old lady like this:

They sat next to each other for several weeks. Clearly they had something in common—they were the only two who had no direct purpose in the playground. They were neither watching grandchildren nor merely sitting on a convenient bench to soak up the sun. They had walked—for the man, at least, this was not so easy—down several levels of steps to reach the playground. Were they staring back at their own youth, a time when their children were walking and tumbling in playgrounds, or were they immersed in even further regression to a time when they themselves were pushing and pulling on doll carriages and toy trucks? The lady sat primly, her neatly ironed dress carefully smoothed beneath her—the man opened the collar button beneath his tie and offered candy to the swarming children. The lady's hands did not fidget in her lap as she held her pocketbook firmly, if not a bit fiercely. They stayed on the same bench, strangers to each other, watching the activity before them—no need or opportunity to exchange a word.

They stayed till the end of each afternoon—till the last few mothers were packing up their belongings and rounding up their by now cranky and dirty children for the walk up the steps, across the Drive and home, somewhere in the large apartment buildings of the immediate nieghhorhood

One day the man said, in his slightly accented voice, "Nice children, nice children, pretty children."

The lady shifted uncomfortably; was he talking to her or was he just speaking, as old people sometimes do—as she found herself doing when washing the coffee cup or reading the paper in the evening? Sometimes she would comment on the news just as if the small apartment were not hers alone.

"You like to watch the children too?" the man asked.

Now there was no mistaking that the question was directed to her, and she answered timidly, "I find I just come here every day as if I had to—it's a nice place, a playground."

The man nodded his head. "In the winter when it's too cold to come, I miss it, don't you?"

"I will this winter," said the lady. "I just moved here." Why had she told him that? She hadn't meant to say anything so personal, so provoking of his confidences, and yet she had said it—"I just moved here."

"Oh," answered the old man, "I lived down on Eighty-sixth Street for many years. My sons found me a new apartment up here, after their mother died. I didn't want to go on in the same place, you know."

"Of course," she replied. She understood perfectly—she knew he had so much wanted to go on in exactly the same place, but had found it financially impossible.

They lapsed into silence. It was her turn to say something, and suddenly she felt like a young girl on one of her first dates. How, she used to wonder, do you talk to them, what do you say? At last she asked him if he visited his sons often. The minute she said it she was sorry—too personal, too direct.

He didn't answer immediately. "They live in the country— one teaches in a college upstate, the other, he has a business in the country. It's a long trip, and then they're busy people, my children. I'm proud of both—" but beneath the words she heard the truth as she herself knew it. There was no friendship or comfort across the generations.

"Are you well?" he asked.

She said, "Yes, pretty well." The heart pains were to be expected. The stomach troubles, coming as they did every few days, were disturbing, but the doctor had checked her and found nothing special wrong. He had suggested she go back to work. She could still teach remedial reading or work in a special school for handicapped children. There they would not mind if she was over the retirement age. But she hadn't wanted to go back to work. She almost hated the doctor when he suggested it—so many years of getting up early, working all day, fighting and caring—so many years of getting supper and cleaning the house, and then nursing him when the arthritis came and the disease. Now she just wanted to do things for herself. To sit in the sun and take care of herself, that's what she wanted. Her giving time was over. She was sure it wasn't idleness that was giving her diarrhea.

She looked over at her companion on the bench. He was not an educated man. She could tell that by the newspaper he carried. It was the kind of scandal sheet she would still never buy. "Do you live near here?"

"Not too far," he said. "I walk the six blocks up and then I take the Broadway subway home. I stop off at the bakery every day and buy cake for dinner." He smiled at her now, the first time he had looked directly at her. She was not a plain woman, and her makeup was still impeccable, her hair perfectly tinted and curled. He wanted to ask her for supper, but a stranger on a park bench, he was afraid of frightening her away. The sun was less brilliant and some of the mothers were already taking their children away. The old man said, "Will you be coming tomorrow?"

"Probably," said the lady. "I come very often"—just as if they had not been seeing each other for weeks.

He had already been ill, she could see when she looked intently at him; one side of his face was slightly paralyzed and he used a cane, now resting on the bench beside him. She had seen him walking slowly and with a limp. He probably won't last long, no sense in my making friends. She was going to pick herself up and go home when he said, "I have some cheese in my icebox and I would be honored to have you come home with me." He almost whispered the last sentence. He turned his head away. His skin was pale and puffy, his bald head was mottled, his blue eyes nearly watered from the efforts he had just made. Years ago his wife had called him a flirt—he had made her unhappy by charming other ladies at parties; now he no longer knew if he had the same touch—if they wouldn't laugh at his pretensions and despise him for his physical feebleness. He wouldn't have dared to ask the lady to come home with him, but day after day he had sat near her and she, too, had watched the children, watched him give the children their candy. He felt her waiting, or was that vanity or false memories? A nerve in his cheek twitched as he waited for her answer.

The lady on her part was taken aback. She smoothed her already perfect hair. It was dangerous to go with strangers and to be picked up in the park. She had thought a thing like that would never happen to her. She had thought no man would look at her again, and though she still put makeup on and creamed her face, it was from years of personal discipline, not from expectation, that she went through those daily rituals. Dinner she had eaten alone ever since he had entered the hospital for the last time, and it almost seemed too much. Why did he want her to come to his place? Could the man mean her any harm? You read such terrible things in the newspapers. She looked over at him. He was staring at the ground, twirling his cane as if her answer was not of any importance to him.

"All right," she said, "I'd like very much to have dinner with you," and so they rose and left the playground a little earlier than usual. They walked slowly up the steps to Riverside Drive. He could not see perfectly even with his glasses, and the world beyond a few feet ahead of him blurred, but he took the lady's arm and leaned on her, as he simultaneously gave the impression that he was conducting her up the stairs. She would miss the early show tonight, but for once it did not matter. She asked him what his favorite television program was, and they talked all the way to the subway station about Garry Moore and Ed Sullivan, about Arlene Francis, and all the spy dramas it turned out they both loved.

Perhaps after this they got into the subway station and he pulled out of his pocket two tokens and paid for her. This pleased her deeply. They were standing together talking as the platform crowded up with people released from work. He saw the ice cream machine, large and red, a few feet away. It was hot underground. "Would you like a Dixie cup?" he asked her.

The lady hesitated. "It would be wonderful." She didn't really want it, she wasn't sure it would agree with her already excited stomach, but she felt it would be wrong to deny her new friend the pleasure of buying her something. She realized now that he wanted to flex his muscles for her. In front of the ice cream machine stood a large black man with an African haircut and a bushy beard. He was with his children, a little boy and girl chewing gum furiously at his side. The old man left his lady's side and moved toward the machine. He didn't see the boy child and he pushed against him.

"Hey," yelled the child, "why don't you watch where you're going?"

The old man was startled. "I'm sorry." He was just reaching in his pocket for a candy for the child when the father stood in front of him.

"You think you can push that child around 'cause he's black. Well, I'm not gonna let ya. Ya white son-of-a-bitch." He moved closer.

"Look, I'm sorry if I hurt the boy. I'm old and I didn't see him."

"You damn well bet you're sorry, just 'cause his skin is dark, ya can't see him." The children stood frozen to the spot. Their eyes were wide and frightened by their father's anger at the old man. "Ya gotta be white and shining so you don't get stepped on, right?" said the black man, pushing himself nearly against the chest of the old man.

A crowd started to gather, mostly black faces—a few yells, "Give it to 'em, man. Don't let 'em get our kids!" The old man stepped back. His eyes began to roll from side to side. The black man came closer. "What ya wanna do, crush all the black babies under your foot? Well, there are some of us that'll get ya first, you're not going to get our black babies."

The old man took another step back, he dropped his cane, his weak leg buckled under him and he was at the edge of the platform. Suddenly the black man moved forward again, and the old man was over the edge and crashed down on the tracks below. They managed to stop the oncoming train and there was a delay of some forty minutes until the ambulance came and took the old man to the hospital. He was unconscious from fright or the impact of his fall. The lady went home and fixed herself soup and a sandwich in her kitchenette and watched the early show exactly as she had originally intended.

. . .

Maybe that's why the old couple are not in the playground today. The baby is sleeping, his pudgy hands hanging down from the edge of the stroller. When I look at him I feel pride and love racing about in my brain causing me to flush and grow hot and my heart to beat loud. After all, I can't build a bridge across a jungle and plant a city. I can't make statues or ten-foot paintings that will hang in the museum. I can't start a factory or discover a new element. I can't equate the universe in a new mathematical relationship. I can't design new furniture or fashion. But I can make another human being. Like the urban poor, the peasant, the serf, the slave, my final defiance is the creation no authority can prevent—a birth.

Elizabeth wants some money for ice cream. The vendor is parked just outside the playground gates. She could go out alone, but she'd never be noticed among the crowd pressing against the white wagon. She's still too small to negotiate this purchase and while I know I shouldn't feel that way, I'm glad. Some day we'll have lunch together and maybe go to the movies in the afternoon. Maybe she won't hate me for whatever she will become. Maybe she'll enjoy talking with me, shopping with me—of course that sounds like an idle daydream or bromide or barbiturate to get through the day. I've never known a mother and daughter who've achieved it, but despite the evidence, I hope still Elizabeth and I will grow trusting each other, being similar and different, being a part but not the entirety of each other. Across such a rivalry, such an inequality of power, such a difference of need, maybe we'll still make a thing between us that neither of us has to be ashamed of, so that we don't have to dread the voice of each other. Can she and I manage a balance in being apart that does not tumble into being alone?

There's the old man with his bag of candy. He was just a little late today. He sits down on a bench and mops his brow with a big handkerchief. He's holding the *Daily News*, but he doesn't read it. He's watching the children.

Tonight we're going to see two Marx Brothers movies at the New Yorker Theater. It will be wonderful to get out of that hot apartment and into the air-conditioned theater. It will be fun to walk along Broadway in the early evening. Everyone is on the street at night: the college students, the nuns taking summer courses in the new math, the old refugee couples who never grew accustomed to their situation, the Israeli musicians who come here to study and never go home, the little old ladies with rolled-up stockings and faded flower hats who live on relief in the hotels tucked in the side streets. The street is perfect in all its extremes. I love walking back after the movie, stopping for pizza or papaya juice at the corner of 103rd Street. I feel on my own land—at least I feel that way when Paul is with me. When I'm alone it's different. I see only the ugly faces then and they seem menacing.

OUT OF WEEK FIVE

When the confirmation came through on the Graduate Department's formal stationery, I was so excited I nearly left my
briefcase at Chock Full o'Nuts, where I had stopped for a
quiet cup of coffee before returning home. I had been chosen
to join Dr. Beineke on an expedition into the interior of the
Amazon to do a six-month study on the primitive Itwo who
survived in near–Stone Age purity on the banks of the river's
interior. As an instructor in anthropology and a woman with
only one small monograph to my name, I was doubly flattered
to have been included in Dr. Beineke's party. I told Paul
immediately after the children were in bed, and we talked
long into the night. He urged me to accept. He reminded me
that we had entered marriage as equal minds, each with a
career the other respected. He and Elizabeth and the baby
would have to let me go for a short time—the experience was
too important to pass up. I wanted to disagree but I knew I
would resent the missed opportunity the rest of my life, and so
on the following day I notified the department that I would be
prepared to leave with the others. Paul and I made arrange-

ments with my mother and the housekeeper, and after a long plane trip, a few nights in a cheap motel and a hot ride in an old Buick, I found myself with Dr. Beineke and Dr. Lawrence, Peter Schwartz and Honor Lindermann (graduate students whose course work was completed), and my friend, Associate Professor Steven Alps, in canoes, with provisions, guides and a small motor launch at the mouth of the Amazon.

It is impossible to describe the wild beauty of the river and the sense of wonder and fear the plant and animal life gave us all—as if we were traveling not over the surface of the globe but down into its center, backward in time to a moment when nature was totally superior to man, man just another of its babbling senseless creatures. No matter how many notes we took—Peter Schwartz photographing everything his eyes could see, Honor sketching the garibus, the red howling monkeys, the capybaras darting into the high grasses of the upper banks—no matter how we tried to set up categories of observation, prepare attitude-analyses of Itwo family structure, whatever we did as we sat gliding over the cabbage leaves and glossy weeds, we knew we were diminishing in size, as the awesome natural world dwarfed and consumed our hard-won intellects, our polished individualities, till we became no more than slithering life moving with the other cellular structures up and down the stream. Sprays of yellow and pink orchids clinging to logs startled us. Begonias, amaryllids, iris, weaving around the fig trees and garlic shrubs, all caught our fascinated attention. Passionflowers, begoniaed vines, papayas, chocolate trees, pipers, ferns, cacti, all reaching up toward the green canopy formed by the giant trees beneath the brilliant blue sky. At sundown the first night we heard the cry of the toucan, a sad wail, a protest against time and place.

Hawks and eagles screamed back and parakeets fluttered about our heads. The tartoruga turtles bumped against our boats and as we walked near our campsite by the shore, a million lizards crossed our path, consuming a billion insects too small to see. Morningside Heights, Riverside Drive, Broadway—a light-year or two away from them all, we sat close together by the campfire. Dr. Beineke told us stories of other expeditions he had led, and reminded us of the need for scientific, objective observation, not emotional reactions, culture-biased and anthropologically invalid. At last we fell asleep, each of us in his own single sleeping bag, a green water-repellent cocoon not nearly as hard as the turtle's shell or as protective as the armadillo's scales.

It took us eight days to reach the swampy marshlands that formed the border of the Itwo territory. During that time we grew more accustomed to the jungle, to the river and to the chores of survival: cooking, cleaning, guarding the provisions from marauding tapirs and squirrels all became routine and we hardened into a close-knit group, a tribe of our own with a leadership system and work-distribution order as simple and yet as rigid as that of any of the tribes we had ever studied in depth. The Itwos were suspicious of strangers, we had been told, due to several unfortunate experiences in their past history in which the white man and his wonderful gun had taken unfair advantage of the local natives whose arms consisted only of stone hammers and bows and arrows, occasionally treated with lethal herbs. Our guide, whose origins were vague, had earned the friendship of the Itwos through many trading journeys. He had brought to them several white government officials and a missionary who had paused only long enough to bless all the heathen, and a health team the government had sent the preceding spring to vaccinate the children. All these intrusions had been peaceful and we hoped that our visit also would pass without any hostility.

The first Itwos we saw (all men) were bathing in the river. The instant they noticed us they disappeared into the grass above. Our guide called to them, but his voice echoed beneath the great trees as in an empty chamber. We beached the canoes and pulled the motor launch, piled high with our provisions and gifts, above the water level. We waited. We waited in the Amazon, feeling more alone with each passing hour. Each of us began to think of human connections left behind, of childhood memories of crowds, like being at the World's Fair, or being given an ice cream stick by a stranger at Coney Island.

Dr. Beineke, sensing the failing courage of his crew, told stories of an archeological dig in Crete where, as a young man, he had found, many centuries down into the ground, a long piece of string that he was convinced (though of course he could not scientifically document the theory) was Theseus' thread, given to him by Ariadne to enable him to escape the Minotaur. We would all have wanted, as the hours turned to dusk and we lit our fire and prepared the evening's meal of K-rations, we would all have wanted a thread to lead us back to civilization as we knew it, muggings, purse-snatchings, bombings, ideological wars, genocide, the whole cluster of activities that make a scientific society, welfare abuses and toilets—all of it seemed preferable to the vacant Amazon where we quietly sat so close to the beginning of history.

When night had totally taken over, we lit our small kerosene lamps and sat together quietly hand in hand like good children in nursery school. Suddenly there appeared around us many naked black bodies adorned with clay bracelets and smeared with the ocher colors that can be squeezed from the center of flowers. We heard women's voices chattering like the little monkeys that swung above our heads all day. The men, holding bows and arrows, stared at us unsmiling and our guide stood up and spoke to them. We all understood some Itwo; we had learned it in the last eight days. We were relieved to catch the word "friend" from the oldest man we saw, and Dr. Beineke stood up and, taking some gaily colored pots and pans, made in Japan, purchased at the Woolworth's on Broadway, he presented them to the Itwo leader. There was much laughter, much smiling. I could see that many of the adults had missing teeth. We all stood up and spoke our names aloud to our new friends and the black Amazon night. It was agreed that we would stay awhile among them, to learn from them how to live well by the river. They were flattered by the request and, I think, as beguiled by the interested warm smile of Dr. Beineke as any of the freshman students that crowded his anthropology classes and clamored for private appointments all during the school year. The Itwos, fascinated by our sleeping bags, climbed into them and stood up in them, jumping about like children in the potato-sack race at a county fair. Certainly our first impressions were of a joyful people in whom the problems of survival, the universal fears of death and destruction had not prevented the development of pleasure. As we fell asleep that night, we all looked forward to the months' work ahead.

The next day the Itwos took us to their village and we began by quietly watching the morning's activities, smiling at the children, holding in our arms some of the babies, who had indeed a strong smell. (The Itwo mothers used a crust of hardened feces about the baby's bottom to protect it from insect bites.) Dr. Beineke instructed us not to take notes publicly for a time, but to return to our campsite in the late afternoon and then write down everything. We watched the women prepare meals, nurse children, strip bark, gather fruit and cook leaves in earthen pots suspended over pit fires. We saw old women picking at the hair on their skin and the men skinning the squirrels and other rodents they had hunted in the early morning. Gradually, as the days passed, we learned more and more of the language, and the faces of the Itwo became distinct and connected to names, and we became less objects of interest and curiosity and more and more helpers and friends. Steven and Dr. Beineke, whose language gifts are extraordinary, were soon able to question the hunters about techniques, and food sources, and even began to learn some of the magic practices. We all heard the dancing and singing, and even the slower ones among us, by the end of the third week, were able to join in some of the repetitive ritualistic songs. We were observers, outsiders, supported by our own group and by the long conversations we held each night about our new friends.

But there grew to be problems among us. Steven wanted very much to continue the gay bachelor existence he so much enjoyed on the Upper East Side of New York with a nubile young tribeswoman who had taken to trailing him during the day and shrieking with provocative laughter every time he turned around to look at her. Dr. Beineke felt that there must be no interfering with normal tribal sexual patterns, not to mention the possibility of unpleasantness should anyone in the tribe feel Steven's presumption out of line. Steven grumbled and groused, but accepted the taboo in the interest of his future anthropological career. Honor ran a fever for a week and we had to nurse her back to health with hot tea and ampules of penicillin. The Itwo allowed Peter to take their pictures and clowned about for him happily. But one day a young blood named Sori jumped from a chocolate tree down on Peter's back just as he was changing film. The camera crashed to the ground and the lens shattered on a stone. Peter was inconsolable, despite the fact that we had prudently brought along a second camera. The first, apparently, like the loved dog of childhood, was irreplaceable.

The women grew to be especially friendly with me and Dr. Lawrence. She in middle age had a stout figure they continually poked at and admired in our communal baths. The Itwos, by contrast, were all thin and spidery, with long breasts with large smooth brown nipples that pointed down toward their toes, like the rich fruit that hung from the high trees.

Zena, a girl of sixteen or so, was very pregnant when we arrived, and I made a special point of befriending her, because my area of interest was passage rites. This includes of course birth and all the drama around it. I worked hard on my language limitations and soon was able to find out who the father-to-be was and what special prenatal care Zena was being given by the older women, who would often slap her naked behind hard as she passed by, or pinch her cheeks till she cried. I found this was common practice among the Itwos with a first pregnancy to help prepare the girl for the pains of motherhood. Sometimes the older women would make Zena hold out her arm while they pierced the skin with arrowheads sharpened like thin blades. Despite the rough treatment her condition brought her, sometimes Zena would look at me, placing her hands on her large belly. She would smile broadly and say "Chix, chix," the Itwo word for "baby."

Despite the general friendliness and mutually warm relations we shared with the Itwo tribe, they held aloof from us in certain areas. We were not allowed on the sacred grounds where they worshiped their ancestors. They would tell us nothing of the practices that took place in this not too distant part of the wood. They allowed us to participate only in total tribal ceremonies, not in the secret events when the leaders, or small groups of men, would disappear to the Abo (the sacred clearing in the forest). Even though this knowledge was crucial to our ultimate understanding of these people, Dr. Beineke did not feel it necessary or possible to push in this area. His hope was that in time we would win the complete confidence of the Itwo, and then be accepted as full tribe members, able to share in the secrets of the group. Unfortunately, this was never to happen, although it seemed to be starting when Zena told me I might come with the others when she had her baby. I was not so excited as to miss the disapproving looks given me by some of the older women who had obviously been against admitting me to such a private event. Further, I realized that Zena had indeed been trusting when she invited me along when I learned that women gave birth on the sacred ground, or Abo, and that only at these times were females permitted in that area. I was warned by Dr. Lawrence, who had heard it from some of her confidants in the tribe, that I would be considered by the older people a possible source of danger for the mother and the child, as the gods might be angry at my trespassing on sacred Itwo ground.

About a week later, as the women were weaving long palm

leaves into fishing nets, Zena suddenly screamed and the
entire Itwo community learned that labor was beginning. I
went with Zena, her mother and three older women, walking
the half mile deep into the forest till we came to the Abo, a
clearing with a flat stone in its center and a single blue circle
painted on the stone. We women quickly made a bed of leaves
for Zena, whose face began to show the strain of slow contractions. She was given two stones to hold in her hands, and a bit
of the bark of a tree was placed in her mouth so she could bite
down hard. The father-to-be came and sat with his back to the
women, his father and some other men of the tribe sitting with
him. Two large fires were lit and then, except for the screech-
ing of the monkeys, the calls of the birds, and the heavy
breathing of Zena, who still had time between contractions,
everything was silent. The sun went down, and the Itwo men
lit torches and placed them in the ground near Zena so the
baby's first moments would not be in darkness. Gradually the
contractions came closer together. Zena had entered the second
stage of labor. She screamed and sobbed and called for her
mother and rolled and tossed as the women held her down.
The men started a chant, a low monotonous rhythm, which
swelled through the forest like rolling waves on the ocean.
Zena seemed to calm down with the sound of the chanting, and
we all seemed to move around to its rhythm. At last her third
and final stage of labor began, the cervix parted for the head,
and the women held her legs apart, and they all screamed and
shouted in words unintelligible to me, and one of the women
went down on her knees and pulled out the baby, dripping
with the blood of passage, his cord fat and blue and shining in
the firelight. The women surrounded the baby so I couldn't see

its sex. I had not heard, in the melée, its cry. The men waited silently. Suddenly one of the old women shouted in anger and pointed toward me. She held the baby up and I saw a hole the size of a half dollar in its chest wall and esophagus; I saw a hand with no fingers and an odd face hanging limp from the neck—a birth abnormality. What now, I thought, and saw the crowd turn toward me, the men walking stiffly. I was the intruder—it was my presence at the Abo the gods had resented; I must be punished. I understood the meaning, if not all the precise words, and began to run toward our campsite. Fortunately the Itwo were not permitted to leave the Abo area without chanting a long ritual prayer first. This gave me time to run almost to the protection of my colleagues. I heard the Itwos behind me; I felt a stinging sharp pain in my neck and stumbled toward our campsite. It seemed that safety and friends were a million miles away. I could hear the Itwos calling out behind me and my legs got heavier and heavier as if I were turning to stone. I forced my muscles to move and dragged on until I saw my friends just ahead. I screamed. Dr. Beineke, Steven, Dr. Lawrence, turning, saw me, and hearing the Itwo close behind, pulled out from our supplies the previously hidden guns and fired high into the jungle tops. The sound stopped the Itwo. They knew what it was. The Amazon was quiet. Dr. Lawrence removed the arrow from my neck, but I could feel the poison seeping through my body. I felt my tongue getting thick and heavy. She poured alcohol in the wound. I tried to explain what had happened in the Abo, but I'm not sure I could make myself understood. Dr. Beineke ordered a rapid evacuation of the campsite. Everything was packed in the canoes, and the canoes strung together attached to the motor launch. As we heard the Itwos, gathering their courage, move once again forward, my friends carried me into the motor launch and we started back down the Amazon, looking for civilization, for medical help.

.   .   .

Today I am able to write this, even to sit up and watch the river gliding by. But my fever is high. Paul, my darling, if I make it home to you, I will never leave you again. I will have adventure enough on the late late show on television. I'll play Jane to your Tarzan only in our own bed. I will learn to bake bread and make chocolate mousse. If I die (I heard Steven say I had only a small chance of survival), please forgive me, darling, I love you.

IN WEEK SIX

Today is hot. Each July I'm surprised again by the weight of the air, and I find my breath is short. I felt somewhat dizzy as I went down the steps from the Drive to the playground. Now I am sitting on the bench feeling heavy, like a turnip buried in the earth. The baby waves bye-bye and goes off to crawl his important crawls. Elizabeth has a friend and the two of them are whispering in a corner, probably nasty things about another child, like "Nancy is a b.m." Cruel and exclusive, Elizabeth takes to social life like the proverbial duck to his pond. I am sewing up a tear in a shirt of Paul's. I never used to be any good with my hands. I nearly failed shop in junior high school and was barely passable in arts and crafts. I bit my nails and I learned to hold pencils and that's about the extent of my manual efforts. I did not make the poster for the high school dance or bake cookies for the bazaar to raise money for the burned-down Baptist church on the wrong side of the tracks. But lately I have been reactivating my hands, using them in the practice of the essential arts—domestic.

I'm now almost four weeks late—and I don't menstruate

that irregularly. I flow blood easily and my periodicity is splendid, and I am always absurdly proud as well as a little shocked by this monthly performance. Of course, sometimes a cold, an upset stomach, a trip, nervous excitement, may delay the shedding of one wall for another, but four weeks is extreme. Possibly I am pregnant. At the thought, as I say the words to myself, as I write them down, my heart starts to pound. I feel a flush of pleasure and a ridiculous sense of exhilaration—but why? Things are hard enough. There are dishes and diapers and needs sufficient in my home to keep me buried for all the years that even the wildest masochist could desire. But the thought does not disappear, and it does not, despite reason, bring anxiety. X and Y, XX, XY, inside of me, right now as I write, an embryo, a fetus, finally a person. Who needs another person? No matter how talented, beautiful or gifted, the world needs fewer people, more breathing space, more food. My baby is otiose, a social inconvenience. I run to my little boy, interrupting his mouthing of old ice cream wrappers. I hug him. I won't love him less, I'll love him more. I start to plan. We can put Peter in with Elizabeth, and the baby in Peter's room, and I can borrow another crib from Louise, my friend in the building, and it will hardly cost anything at all. Perhaps I should go to the doctor to be sure. Perhaps I should first take a urine specimen to the laboratory on 114th. They'll call Dr. Z. and within six hours I can know. Oh rabbit, friend of mine—enlarge your little nipples, show symptoms of pregnancy, please.

I sit in the sun of my own anticipation for a while. Then another thought destroys my peace. X and Y, XY or XX or maybe XYZ. Mutations do happen: intrauterine second-month

150

development of fangs, green skin, scales. Third intrauterine month, gills, longer fangs, pop eyes, hair on hands, nails sharp, in fact claws, a monster growing in me—a comic book terror building strength from my blood system, and suddenly tearing with its pointed fangs at my uterus, like the chicken at its shell, and shattering my stomach wall open and bleeding; it would leap on to the bed, the embodiment of all that is vicious and ugly within me—the demon that causes bad fantasies personified as my baby. The child that eats up your guts on its way out to the world is not an impossible monster. But what a nightmare I am having. I am sure this third meeting of egg and sperm is developing normal-splendid. A beautiful creature with perhaps a mathematical gift. I've always admired people who can play with abstractions, moving them around in their heads like so many mosaic tiles, building portraits of mental designs so beyond my concrete imagination. My baby can be so many things hidden, recessed in the gene pattern that Paul and I keep secret in our cellular structure. . . . A great-grandfather's violin-playing may result in my child's extraordinary musicality, or a grandmother of Paul's whose legs I have been told attracted all the attention at the church socials may result in a movie star three generations later, and what I really want, what I'm after, is an extension, a selfish extension of my being into more life than I can contain in one—singular—body. I want to expand myself not merely in time, but in space, out toward other connections, to be a multiple person, to experience as much as possible. Now I am allowing myself to be sentimental. Motherhood is always a greedy affair and eventually a suckling-off of the suckler— and it never works out the way it's planned. There's always a fighting and a pull. A mother and offspring on each end of a wishbone, a tugging till victory—the child's, of course: he takes the larger part, gets his wish and runs.

I take Peter smiling at me—his baby hands still exploring my mouth, my nose, pulling at me in rough play. He's dirty all over and triumphant with his new physical skills. I am now the all-powerful, all-necessary center to his narrow universe. I am his servant, his provider, his lover, his goddess, irrational like Jehovah, and yet tender like the Virgin Mary. Sometime in the not so distant future, I will be his enemy. He will flee and I will chase him. Where have you been? You must be home by twelve. No, you may not do that. No, you cannot have money for that. And then it will be like other kinds of love affairs, alternating layers of bitterness and nostalgia—and eventually a minor boredom. "Oh yes, remind me to send my mother a birthday card." And I will worship him, and even should he prove a disaster, I will carry mementoes and pictures, keep all his school reports and athletic awards. And at the end it will all be burned as rubbish when someone sorts through my private effects looking for stock market certificates and things like that that old ladies are always stashing away in hat boxes. But it doesn't matter about the end—the process is so important. (He pulls at my sandal as if to unbuckle the leather strap.) Like a medieval jousting session, the rituals that cover the fierce combat of mother-child love are magnificent, and I enter the battle joyfully, though it stretch ahead for years, because it's the only arena to really test my mettle, to shape my reputation, to give me a self whose colors I will wear with pride.

Elizabeth has come to me with a demand that I push her on the swing. I am tired of doing things. I want to stay in my own thoughts, but she's beginning to whine, sensing my withdrawal, and I will have to go, since discipline in one's work means subjugating whims and impulses, self, to higher plans. I will be disciplined, get up from this bench and go to the swings, my feet passing through the steam rising from the cement. I am a guru, an Indian yogi. I can sit on a bed of nails and walk through fire, because I can concentrate on God and exclude all other sensations. No, I cannot concentrate on God. I find when I try I only brood about myself. Elizabeth, I am coming to the swings. Tomorrow first thing I will take a urine specimen to the laboratory. Will Dr. Z. be surprised to hear from me again?

I push Elizabeth on the swing and she kicks her feet in pleasure. Her small brown sandals are scuffed and in need of a polishing they will never get. I'm perspiring from the activity and there are wet dark circles under the armholes of my cotton dress. I think of Elizabeth lying on a bed some many years from now, a boy, a man, awkwardly spreading her legs apart, touching her, and she, not knowing how to stop, how to prevent the vacuum of time from sucking her up, will lie passive and be consumed, and as I think of the heat and sensation of her body rolling on the sheets, in sex, in labor, in illness and in death, I feel a great exhaustion, a fatigue of certain defeat—that's all that can possibly come of the days I spend in the park expecting secretly the playground concrete to crack and wild orchids to push their way up to the sunlight, and lizards to dash between the slide and the swing, and nature to change back to an Eden before the apple, where Paul and I can live without erosion in perpetual beauty.

I know that we have been condemned to a simple life of increasing compromises. I know that minor hatreds and petty resentments will come more and more between us. Paul, Elizabeth, Peter, the new baby and I will grow closer and closer in memories of days that promised more than they gave and love that offers everything and then like a mirage disappears as we get closer. But what else can I do but listen to myself as I prepare chicken in wine sauce for the friends we will have to dinner tomorrow night, read Elizabeth a book about Raggedy Ann and how she got her candy heart that says "I love you" sewed right into the middle of her chest—what else can I do but tell Paul that I have not given up all hope for a revolution that will not be corrupt . . . a barricade can still be erected behind which saints may stand? I must believe evolution is not complete. I'll take Peter to the five and dime and buy him a stuffed elephant like the one he wanted to take from the carriage parked next to ours.

OUT OF WEEK SIX

———•·◦∞◦·•———

I am definitely pregnant. Paul is uneasy but will get over his anxieties in time. He's also very proud of his extraordinary fertility. We are, he says, a social unit, the two of us, our children. We are part of history. We give ourselves a second chance for perfection. We are doing what the Neanderthals, the Indians, the Babylonians and the Assyrians, the Egyptians and the Hittites, the Tartars and the Mongolians, the Indo-Europeans, and the Twelve Tribes of Israel have all done. We will not be spun off the planet's surface, unlinked to our kind. Last night he told me, as I was standing naked, folding our bedspread, that I was beautiful. This morning I caught him admiring his body in the mirror, tapping his penis with pride, the way you reward a horse for a race well run.

I hope the baby will be healthy and undamaged.